# Kyle's Passion

A Novel

by

## Cassandra J. Sperry

ISBN **978-0615880464**

Second Edition

# KYLE'S PASSION

My Knight,

Your shield (love) protects me daily from the many arrows (ups and downs) I must cope with.

Your Lady Love

# PROLOGUE

As Abby unlocked the door to her future husband's apartment she couldn't believe she was to be married in a month. She had arrived at Richard's earlier than she had intended to so she could make supper for him, which consisted of steak, baked potatoes, corn, and for dessert she had made a Devil's food cake.

While she checked for the supper items that she had asked Richard to get, she thought about the wedding arrangements that her mother and Richard's mother were making.

Her wedding colors were coral and ivory. Andrea, her twin sister, and her bridesmaids would be wearing coral floor length, sleeveless satin gowns; the gowns had thin straps and embroidered tranquil bodices. Abby's wedding dress was of course white; a strapless A-line gown with delicate embroidery and beading around the bodice and skirt that buttoned down the back; underneath she would wear a white petticoat and adorning her thick, silken black hair would be an oval cut, plain edge veil with blusher, scattered with crystals and pearls. To hold it in place was a four- inch satin covered comb.

Richard had proposed on Valentine's Day and wanted her to graduate from high school before they were married. There had only been five months to make the wedding arrangements. He hadn't wanted to wait because of his position at Dalton Law Offices.

The wedding would take place at the city of Shelby's popular Memorial Park overlooking the river. The reception would be inside the nearby pavilion.

In her mind's eye Abby pictured the park filled with seating for the guests during the ceremony. The dining tables in the pavilion were adorned with ivory tablecloths, coral crepe paper draped around the edges. The sides of the pavilion would be colored with coral and ivory to make it festive and cozy.

Coming out of her musings, she looked at the cake she had made the night before. She smiled remembering how Richard had tried coaxing her into making love while she'd mixed the batter.

"Richard, we only have to wait a month and then we can make love anytime." Abby told him.

"A month is a lifetime. I want to show you how much I love you now." He'd said.

"I want our wedding night to be perfect. Please understand I want my first time making love to be special, magical." Abby reminded him.

He had kissed her and told her he understood, but let her know her refusal wasn't something he'd accept once they were married.

Hearing noises coming from the bedroom, Abby went to investigate. Without making a sound, she cautiously opened the door.

After witnessing her fiancé in bed with her best friend, she let out a small cry of disbelief. Abby turned around, embarrassed at having caught them in a moment of passion.

Richard heard her and looked in her direction saying, "It isn't as bad as it looks."

Abby turned to him. "You two-timing bastard." She turned toward Jessie, who looked away in fear. "How could you? I didn't believe the rumors everyone spread about you." She said.

She took Richard's ring off, throwing it at him and put his apartment key on his dresser, then turned and ran blindly out of the apartment. Running in the front door of her parents' home, she yelled, "Mama!" Judy Phillips came out of the kitchen. "You look like you've lost your best friend." Judy said.

"Mama, it's Richard and Jessie." Abby said collapsing and beginning to sob in her mother's waiting arms.

Judy held her until the sobs turned into hiccups.

"Now tell me what happened." Judy said, but she already knew.

Abby told Judy what had happened. Abby didn't understand her mother's lack of surprise. She looked at her for a moment.

"You knew, didn't you Mama? Before I told you, you knew." Abby accused. "Why didn't you tell me?"

"Yes Abby, I knew. I'm so sorry I didn't tell you, but would you have believed me?" Judy said.

Abby thought for a moment. "No." She admitted.

Abby and her mother canceled the wedding arrangements. The invitations, which had taken her a month to decide on, because of her traditional and Richard's contemporary styles, hadn't been sent out. Richard called and dropped by the house numerous times to explain what Abby had seen. She steadfastly refused to have anything to do with him. Several weeks passed while Abby cried and began staying out well past dawn each night trying to put him out of her mind; she wore herself out and put her health in jeopardy.

Finally her mother could watch her no more. Judy called her sister-in- law in Atlanta. Together the two made plans to get Abby away from her hometown of Shelby.

Hell bent on defying her mother's plans to send her to Atlanta, Abby told her she wouldn't go, stating she was an adult and wouldn't be treated like a child. Judy threatened to send her to live with her widowed grandfather if she refused going to Aunt Millie's.

Abby wisely chose to go live with Aunt Millie. She loved her grandfather but since his wife's death two years earlier he'd become cold and distant.

When Abby stepped off the plane in Atlanta Millie was there to greet her.

"This isn't going to work, Aunt Millie." Abby said rebelliously.

"I don't know what you're talking about." Millie lied.

"Yes, you do. Getting me out of Shelby isn't going to change my behavior." Abby stated.

"I need a Personal Assistant, Tabitha. I don't care how you behave." Millie replied. "Let's get you home and settled. I have papers piled to the ceiling."

On the way to Millie's two-story brick house Abby sat tensely in the seat next to her aunt. Millie tried to engage her in conversation. Abby defiantly refused to speak to her aunt.

Millie pulled up in front of the two-story brick house she'd bought forty years earlier after her fiancé had run off without explanation.

After putting away Abby's things, Millie put her straight to work typing. She had slightly exaggerated the pile of papers, but not by much.

Abby had been at her aunt's home for a few days. Putting her to work had changed her behavior; she didn't have time to indulge in self-pity or stay out past dawn each night.

"I think we'll stop here. Have you thought about what you're going to do now that you've cancelled your wedding?" Millie asked.

Standing, and stretching her back, Abby said, "Not really, I hadn't intended to work. We had decided I'd stay home for a few years then start a family."

"Why not consider staying in Atlanta? You can do the typing while I work on more important things." Millie said.

"You know I can't stay here, Aunt Millie. I have to face everyone back home sometime." Abby answered.

"Yes, it was selfishness on my part."

"You selfish? Not likely. You're one of the most selfless people I know. Since we're through for the day do you mind if I go out for a while?"

"Of course not. I'm not a jailer."

"I didn't mean to imply that you were."

"I was teasing you, Tabitha. Go, have a good time. I won't wait up." Abby went to her room. She picked out a gold velveteen top and a pair of stonewashed jeans. She put her make-up on lightly, pulled her hair into a neat French braid, and went to one of the popular clubs near her aunt's home.

# CHAPTER ONE

Coming down the stairs from the upper floor in her parents' two-story home, Abby Phillips turned at the bottom. "I told you I was not going to that damn dance." She stated clearly, in a whiskey smooth voice.

"You have to go. Last year's queen can't crown this year's winner, she broke her leg." Andrea told her. "You're the only past queen here to do it."

While they were talking, the front door opened. Eric Phillips and Kyle Masterson entered.

"They can hear you all the way into town." Eric said.

Abby turned around sharply. "Eric! We didn't know you were coming home." She exclaimed throwing herself at her brother.

She didn't see the man with him; he stood in the shadow of the door. Eric wrapped her in a bear hug. Surprised, Kyle stepped out of the shadow of the door when he saw her.

"If you had known I was coming home it wouldn't have been a surprise." Eric told her.

He turned around to introduce her to Kyle. "Kyle, my sister Abby. Abby, my boss Kyle Masterson."

Eric had let go of her after turning around.

Abby stood rigidly glaring at the man she knew, who gazed back at her from steel, blue-gray eyes. Kyle saw instant recognition in her chocolate brown eyes. She hadn't changed much in the nearly five years since he'd met her. She'd grown more beautiful and was more curvaceous.

Her close-set eyes had been like melted chocolate on an oval face, with a perky, upturned nose and full, round mouth.

"I'm pleased to meet you, Mr. Masterson." She said, surprised to find she sounded normal.

"I'm sure the pleasure is mine, Miss Phillips." Kyle said mockingly, in a drawling baritone.

He was almost a foot taller than her own five seven. His blond hair lay in disarray, looking as though he'd run his hands through it repeatedly. He had a strong, muscular chest that gave way to the flat, smooth line of his stomach and lean hips.

At that moment Judy and Andrea Phillips came down the stairs from the upper floor. Upon seeing her brother, and sparing a glance in his companion's direction, Andrea hurled herself at him much the same way her twin had moments earlier.

"Why didn't you tell us you were coming home?" She scolded in a voice similar to Abby's.

"I wanted to surprise you." Eric said, turning to fold his mother in a hug.

After releasing her, he said, "Mama, my boss Kyle. Kyle, my mother Judy, and my sister Andrea."

"It's nice to finally meet you, Kyle. Eric talks about you so often I feel as if I know you already." Judy said.

And I wish I'd have paid more attention when Eric talked about you. Maybe then I would have been prepared to see you again. Abby thought.

"It's nice to meet you and your lovely daughter, Mrs. Phillips." Kyle said, raising Andrea's hand to his lips.

He met Abby's gaze, nodding when she noticed his deliberate offer of gallantry toward her sister.

Refusing to submit to his challenge, she turned to Eric. "How long will you be home?"

"I'll tell you about it tonight at supper. Right now I want to shower and change." He answered.

"Where are my manners? You must be tired after your trip. Eric, take Kyle up to the guest room. Supper will be ready in an hour." Judy told them.

"Mama is telling us to clean up before supper." Eric said humorously, as he dodged Judy.

She just missed swatting him on the behind as he headed toward the stairs.

"You're not too old to put across my knee, young man." Judy threatened with humor.

"Yes ma'am, this way Kyle." Eric urged leading the way to the guest room.

Abby walked through the snowy meadow behind her family home. Her straight, thick, silken black hair fell past her waist and swung over her shoulder. She pushed it back irritably. She had thought about Kyle often during the nearly five years since she'd met him. "I wish I'd have learned more about Kyle when we met, then maybe I'd have some idea how to handle him." She said aloud.

Abby had learned to conceal her emotions. Seeing Kyle standing in her living room, she had temporarily lost that ability. Quickly recovering, she'd made excuses to get away from him.

She couldn't forget the night she'd met him. She was eighteen and had gone to Atlanta after her broken engagement. She was sitting alone, at a corner table of the club when Kyle walked up to her. "May I have this dance?" He asked and bowed.

She only stared, mesmerized. He reached over, took her hand in his, and led her to the dance floor. While he held her, she unwound. The music flowed through her like water over the falls.

They danced for hours. It seemed they had been together for a lifetime. They didn't need words, only the gentle sway of their bodies.

Acting as though he were becoming bored with the club, he led her outside. It was hot and damp. They walked and talked; talking about things that didn't matter and had only exchanged first names. There would be time later to learn more.

She hadn't had anything harder to drink than Diet Coke. She let him lead her into the lobby of his hotel when they suddenly came upon it. After guiding her to the elevator, and the doors closed, he pulled her to him, kissing her. They arrived on his floor; he walked her along the corridor pursuing his passion. When they came to his room, he inserted the key.

Pulling her into his room, his kisses were full of passion, more than the ones in the elevator had been. He kissed her eyes, her lips. Everywhere he could reach without moving his head much, he kissed.

Abby, having lost the ability to think clearly when he'd asked her to dance returned his passion.

Kyle's hands slid up her back, his mouth moved down her throat to her breast. He suckled the softness through her top until her body arched toward him.

Slowly he undressed her, loving her with his hands and mouth before her naked beauty was exposed to his hungry gaze.

"You're beautiful." He told her, drinking in her nudity.

She wanted to arouse him the way he had her, but he pushed aside her attempts, saying, "Let me love you."

He let her help him take off his clothes. Somehow they had gotten to the bed. How had they gotten there? She didn't know, much less care. Her body arched up to meet his. He pulled away.

"Please love me." Abby pleaded, holding her hands out to him.

"I assure you my love I'll do more than love you." Kyle said.

He got up to remove a foil packet from his luggage. He opened it and sheathed himself. He was back before her heated body had a chance to register the coolness of the room.

Kneeling between her thighs, he tenderly kissed her lips. When she was at the edge again, he thrust into her quickly and smoothly.

He barely had time to ascertain that he was her first lover before her climax began. Moving with gentleness, tenderness he loved her. His culmination brought renewed waves of pleasure to her.

"You should have told me." He said when she lay within the circle of his arms.

"Would it have mattered?" She asked.

"No, but I might have hurt you in my...passion." He said.

"You didn't hurt me." She assured him.

He laid his fingers against her lips. "Hush, go to sleep, Love. We'll talk in the morning."

In the morning, no we won't talk in the morning I won't be here. She thought.

Assuring herself he was asleep, she dressed and left his room. She was frightened, so left him to wake up alone and went back to Aunt Millie's. Without explanation to her aunt, she packed, called a taxi to take her to the airport, exchanged her ticket for an earlier flight and flew home. Without intention to, she'd had her special, magical wedding night without benefit of the wedding.

The man who had turned her world upside down was staying in their guest room.

Andrea had seen the look that passed between Kyle and Abby. She knew her sister would be walking in the meadow. Whenever Abby wanted to be alone, that's where she went.

When she caught sight of Abby, Andrea saw a fleeting glimpse of fear in her brown eyes. In a moment it was gone.

Abby spotted Andrea a moment after she'd seen her. Putting on a radiant smile, she met her halfway.

"Mama sent me to get you, she wants us to help with supper." Andrea said.

They walked in silence for a moment.

"Kyle's the man you met in Atlanta after you broke your engagement, isn't he?" Andrea asked.

"How did you know?" Abby asked.

"I saw the way you looked at each other. You told me about him when you came home from Aunt

Millie's...remember? I put two and two together." Andrea said.

"I don't know why Kyle is here, but I won't let him turn my world upside down again." Abby stated.

"What makes you think he will?"

"He does. I can't explain it. I feel something when I'm near him...a connection."

"You don't want to get involved, you're afraid he does."

"Yes."

"Not all men are like Richard. They can be faithful."

"I'll have to take your word for it. I'm not fool enough to put myself through that kind of pain again."

Andrea gazed at her sister with piercing emerald eyes. "You can't mean that you're distrustful of all men."

They'd reached the house. Grateful for the reprieve, Abby went inside.

"Is something wrong, Abby?" Judy asked when she and Andrea went in.

They helped with supper.

"No, I was just wishing spring would come; it seems like we've had winter forever." Abby fibbed.

"Spring will be here soon enough. I remember when you were a little girl; you could hardly wait for the flowers to bloom. You'd run in the meadow just to feel the grass beneath your feet." Judy said.

Abby laughed. "I haven't changed. I feel as though I've been lying dormant, and when the flowers bloom, so do I."

"You always thought by running through the flowers you'd be as beautiful as they were." Andrea reminded her.

"Spring seems so magical, everything comes alive. It reminds me of love and romance. People and places long forgotten, come back anew.

I've always wanted to start a new romance in spring." Abby said wistfully.

"Maybe you can. Kyle could be just what you're dreaming of." Andrea suggested.

Abby glared at her. "Maybe." She pretended to be engrossed in mashing potatoes.

"I do believe Abby has fallen in love, Mama." Andrea teased. "Andie, that's ridiculous. I just met the man." Abby lied.

"Stranger things have happened. Besides,  you need a man in your life." Andrea stated.

"Don't you have anything better to discuss than my love life?"  Abby asked irritably.

"Or lack of." Andrea commented.

"Andrea, go call everyone to supper." Judy ordered.

"Yes Mama." She said as she walked out of the kitchen.

When Abby entered the dining room she saw that Kyle had been seated to the right of her chair.  She was left-handed, Kyle was right.  She looked suspiciously at Andrea, but was ignored.

She walked stiffly to her father's side. Bending, she kissed his cheek. "Hello, Daddy.  How was work today?" She asked.

"Work was fine, Tabi. Your mother tells me you still refuse to attend the Spring Ball." Andrew said.

"Yes, we've already discussed this." She said, taking her seat next to Kyle.

"I have asked you to reconsider. You're young you shouldn't be hiding in the house. You should be looking for a young man to settle down with." Andrew commanded.

Abby felt Kyle stiffen beside her.

Andrew noticed the change in their guest. He smiled inwardly.

"Andrew, the supper table is not the place to discuss this." Judy told him.

"All right, love." Andrew agreed.

He warned Abby with his eyes they would discuss it later.

After supper it was decided to have coffee in the study. Judy excused herself to clean up. Andrew told her to leave it until later. Obeying her husband's command, Judy took coffee into the study.

"How long will you be home Eric?" Andrew asked.

"A week." Eric told him.

At Judy's look of dismay, he continued, "Kyle and I have to return to Atlanta in a week. Kyle has hired me to run the new division of K. M. Enterprises in Shelby."

"Just what I need! Kyle traveling back and forth between Shelby and Atlanta!" Abby mumbled to herself.

"Did you say something, Tabi?" Andrew asked.

"No sir." She answered.

"You're coming home?" Judy asked hesitantly.

~ 15 ~

"Yes Mama, I'm coming home." Eric answered.

"Won't it be good to have our boy home, Andrew?" Judy said tearfully.

"About time too." Andrew grumbled.

"Will you be here for the Spring Ball?" Andrea demanded excitedly.

"I had planned on it. Why, do you need a date?" Eric teased.

"Of course not. I have a date thank you." Andrea said.

"Speaking of the ball, Miss Tabi I suggest that you rethink your decision not to attend." Andrew said.

"I've made my decision, Daddy. But if it means that much to you I'll think about it again." Abby told him.

"I hope so...after all the time your mother spent making your gown." Andrew told her.

Abby's eyes widened, she turned to her mother. "You made a gown for me?" She asked.

Judy returned her look, silently pleading with Abby to comply with her father's wishes.

"I made it in case you changed your mind." Judy told her. Abby walked over to take her coat off the coat rack.

"If you'll excuse me, I'm going to get some air." She said as she put her coat on.

"Why won't she attend the ball? Does she still resent Richard because of their broken engagement?" Eric asked.

"She doesn't resent him now. She won't allow herself to get involved. If she goes to the ball there's a

chance that will happen. Closing herself off is safer."
Andrea told him.

"That doesn't sound like Abby." Eric said.

"Ever since she came back from Aunt Millie's so quickly she hasn't dated a lot. Something happened to her, she won't say what it is. Says it's our imagination whenever we bring it up." Andrea told him, only half lying.

Kyle tensed at Andrea's statements. He had to find out why Abby ran away from him in Atlanta. She had been warm and more than receptive to his lovemaking. She'd made light of the fact that she'd been a virgin. He was going to get some answers from her if he had to shake them out of her. He stood up.

"If you don't mind I'd like to try talking to her. It might be easier for her to talk to a stranger." He told Andrew.

"She can be stubborn, son." Andrew warned.

Kyle nodded his head in acknowledgment, put on his coat, and went in search of Abby. He found her in the meadow. When she heard him approaching she looked anxiously for a place to hide. When she found none, she gave up thoughts of hiding. He sauntered toward her. His long, muscled legs brought him to her quickly.

He had a perfectly chiseled face. His steel, blue-gray eyes were evenly spaced, set apart by a long angular nose, above a soft, sexy mouth. "I suppose my father asked you to come out here." She guessed.

"No, I volunteered. I told him it might be easier if you could talk to a stranger." He corrected.

"You've been my lover you could hardly be considered a stranger." She reminded him.

"Your family doesn't know we've been lovers. Why didn't you tell them we met in Atlanta?" He asked.

"It's none of their business. Andrea knows I met a man in Atlanta, now she knows it was you. I suppose you're going to tell the rest of my family."

"Why did you run away after we made love?"

"What's the big deal? We met, had a few dances and made love."

"Was it a game, Abby?" He pulled her to him.

"I did what any woman would when confronted with a man who exudes sensuality the way you do."

"When I woke up and didn't find you in my room I asked the desk clerk if he'd seen you. Do you know how I felt discovering you'd left after we made love? I searched Atlanta for two days hoping to find you."

He kissed her. She struggled to free herself, but he was stronger. He used that strength. When she became pliant in his arms, he broke off the kiss. "Now tell me it was a game, Abby. Convince me I couldn't have made love to you just now." He said fiercely.

He pulled her to him a second time. She thrust her hands into his hair to pull him closer. Impatiently he pushed off her coat. Pulling her sweatshirt over her head, he trailed hot kisses along her neck to the valley between her firm, supple breasts.

His mouth suckled her through the lacy undergarment that molded her. She arched into his mouth; making soft mewing noises while her hands held him to her.

Kyle's head snapped up when he heard someone approaching. Abby shuddered at the sudden loss of his warm mouth.

"Kyle, please." She reached for him, attempting to pull him back.

"Someone's coming, put your clothes back on." He ordered gruffly. Abby obeyed when she heard the voices.

"We'll continue this later." He promised.

She faced him. "You look as though you've thoroughly been made love to." He told her sheepishly.

"I can promise it won't happen again." Abby hissed.

"Don't make promises you can't keep, Kitten. I will kiss and make love to you again. Although next time, there won't be any interruptions." He vowed.

Abby walked past him to go to the house. She stopped abruptly. Walking toward them were Jessica Goodson and Eric.

Abby began to tremble uncontrollably. Kyle walked up behind her, putting his hands on her shoulders to steady him when he collided with her.

Feeling her trembling, he asked, "What is it, Abby? Are you all right?"

She stood in silence as Eric and Jessica came closer.

"Good evening." Jessie purred.

Abby tried to walk around her brother and traitorous former friend. Kyle observed her intent almost as soon as she started to move. He wrapped his arms around her waist pulling her to him to prevent her escape.

"Beautiful night isn't it? Abby and I were just about to take a walk. Won't you join us?" He said.

"We'd love to, wouldn't we, Darling?" Jessie answered, looking adoringly at Eric.

Abby made another attempt to go around them. Kyle's arms tightened enough to make her gasp.

"I wouldn't advise trying that again. If you do I'll be forced to show Eric and his friend just what they interrupted back there." He whispered for only Abby to hear.

"Kyle, this is Jessica Goodson, Jessica, my boss Kyle Masterson." Eric introduced.

"Pleased to meet you, Jessica." Kyle said, extending his hand toward her.

"I'm sure the pleasure is mine. My friends call me Jessie." She said softly, taking his hand.

He took his hand out of hers when she applied a subtle, implied pressure.

"Among other things." Abby muttered under her breath.

Kyle's hand slid, leaving a warm trail, from her waist to slap her on the bottom. Abby stood rigid.

"What brought you out this evening?" Abby said bitingly.

"Eric and I have been dating for over a year. We decided now was as good a time as any to tell everyone." Jessie said looking directly at Abby.

Eric couldn't look at his sister. He was ashamed of the pain Jessie's announcement may have caused.

"Isn't that just wonderful." Abby said too brightly.

Eric and Jessie didn't detect the sarcasm. Kyle did, it earned her another slap on the bottom. With gentle, firm pressure Kyle urged Abby toward the house, his arms never leaving her waist. She was in no doubt he was still aroused from their earlier confrontation. She felt it against the hip he was using to push her toward the house. Eric and Jessie didn't have any choice but to follow them. When they came to the house, Kyle excused himself. He needed a cold shower, a very cold shower.

Later, unable to sleep as she lay in bed, Abby rose and quietly padded down to the kitchen. Once there she switched on the light. Making hot chocolate, she didn't hear, but felt Kyle when he walked in.

"I thought warm milk helped you sleep." He said.

Abby spun around sharply. "I needed something stronger than warm milk. Didn't anyone ever teach you not to sneak up on others?" She spat.

"I wasn't sneaking. I wasn't able to sleep either so I came to get a drink. Is it my fault you were so engrossed in what you were doing you didn't hear me?" He said lazily, leaning on the door jam. "I noticed you weren't startled by my presence."

"When it comes to you I seem to have a sixth sense. Would you like some hot chocolate?" She said.

"You mean like E.S.P.?"

"No, not E.S.P. I don't want to discuss this. Do you want hot chocolate or not?"

"No, I had something stronger in mind."

"Daddy keeps Scotch in the study. Would you like me to get it for you?"

"No, if you point me in the right direction I can get it myself."

Abby directed him to the study. He came back a few minutes later with the bottle of Scotch walking in to stand next to her. He watched her make hot chocolate. She felt him watching her. The hair on the back of her neck stood up as if a chill had suddenly gone through her, she shuddered.

"Are you cold?" Kyle asked.

"No, if I were it would be none of your concern." She told him tersely.

"Wouldn't it? I was raised a gentleman, to take care of my lover's needs." He told her seductively.

Abby turned toward him. "I am not your lover and you are not a gentleman. Gentlemen do not go around flaunting their affairs. What the hell are you doing here?" She spat.

"We aren't having an affair...yet. I was lying in bed wondering how your former fiancée could have let a tigress like you get away. I heard you get up and followed you. Why haven't you told your family we met after you broke your engagement?"

"We've been over this. How did you know about my engagement?"

"It doesn't matter how I know. The answers you gave didn't satisfy me."

"I was eighteen when we met. I didn't understand how I could make love with you when I had just broken my engagement to the man I thought I loved. I refused to let Richard make love to me until our wedding night.

I let you make love to me shortly after we met. You had me spellbound from the moment you walked up to my table and asked me to dance. It would have been my wedding night."

Kyle sat the Scotch on the counter. "You used me?"

Abby turned away. "No! I went to that club to relax and unwind. I never intended to get involved with another man again."

"What did you think I'd do when I found you in my bed the next morning?"

"I didn't think about the morning. You said we'd talk in the morning. I panicked and ran after you fell asleep. Think of it as another conquest and leave it at that."

Grasping her shoulders, he turned her to face him.

"Another conquest, I don't keep track of the number of women I've bedded. You weren't just another conquest as you call it. You are the only woman I've ever made love to who gave freely of herself and didn't expect anything in return. Have you let another man make love to you?"

"That is none of your business."

Kyle put her between the counter and his solid form. He pressed his lips to hers. Abby struggled until the fire he started burned out of control. Feeling her resistance fading, he darted his tongue into the deep recesses of her mouth.

Pulling away, he asked huskily, "Have you taken another lover?"

"No. How could I when..." She never finished her sentence.

He groaned into her mouth and slowly began making love to her. He kissed her eyes and mouth, down her neck. Finding her cotton nightgown, he undid the buttons with his teeth.

When she was exposed to him he sucked greedily at her supple breasts. She lifted to him, wanting the aching pleasure he gave. His hands busily moved to caress her thighs. He made slow, lazy circles up her thighs to her flat stomach.

She arched toward him begging for release. For long minutes he nipped and bit and touched, not freeing her from his seduction. Kyle brushed his hand across her swollen, aching breasts.

"I've waited nearly five years to make love to you again. I don't intend to wait another five. You belong to me I will not let you run away again." He said hoarsely.

She couldn't believe what she was hearing. Pushing him away, she smoothed down her nightgown.

"You don't own me! I'm not a possession you use and discard when you feel the desire." She fumed.

She started to walk away. He grabbed her around the waist and together they sank to the floor. She lay beneath him.

"Do you want to wake the whole house?" He hissed.

"I don't care if I wake the dead. I'm not going to let you treat me as a toy you play with when you're in the mood!" She spat.

"I want you Abby. I won't keep it a secret." He said then kissed her. She struggled he kissed her passionately. When her body told him she wanted to be loved, he picked her up and carried her to his room. They lay on the bed. Their passion consumed them. He drew out their lovemaking. Abby begged him for release.

"Now, Kyle. Love me now." She pleaded.

He loved her, but not in the way she'd asked. He loved her with his hands and mouth, not allowing her release until she lay exhausted in his arms, falling asleep with his name on her lips.

When she awoke in the morning Abby was horrified to find Kyle in her bed.

"Good morning, Darlin'. Did you sleep well?" He asked.

"What are you doing in my bed? What if someone walks in?" She snapped.

"No one is likely to walk in without knocking. We're in my room." He told her.

"Your room? How did I get here?" She demanded.

"I don't know whether to take that as a compliment or an insult to my lovemaking. Let's just say we got caught up in the heat of the moment."

"We did not make love last night unless you took advantage of me after I fell asleep."

"When I make love to you, you will be well aware of it."

She left Kyle's room without a backward glance. When Abby saw her reflection in the mirror in her bathroom, she grimaced. Everyone would know that she and Kyle had spent the night together. Still that's all they'd done. She was oddly disappointed.

Shouldn't she be happy he hadn't taken advantage of the opportunity he'd had last night?

Stepping into the shower she turned on the water, slowly turning the handle to the right until it was comfortably warm. Standing under the stinging spray she scrubbed her body until it had a healthy, pink glow. Calling herself every kind of fool, Abby replayed in her mind Kyle's lovemaking.

"He's a very dangerous man you would do well to steer clear of him in the future." She reminded herself.

Setting her mind to it she washed her hair until it shone. Coming from the shower draped in a towel she stopped dead. Kyle was standing in the door of her bath.

"What are you doing in here? If someone comes in they'll think..." She trailed off.

"They'll think what Abby? That we made love last night?" He growled.

"Get out of her before someone comes in." She begged.

"Did you hope to avoid me?" He asked bitterly. His eyes were a steel-blue glint.

"I don't want them to get the impression that..."

"That we're lovers. I intend to make it known that you are mine. I'm giving you until the end of the day to tell your family about us." He announced.

"If I refuse?" She returned coldly.

"Arrangements can be made to make our relationship look, shall we say, less than respectable."

"You wouldn't dare! Our relationship isn't sleazy. It's..."

"It's what Abby?"

She couldn't bring herself to say the words. "You are a despicable bastard."

"You're changing the subject Love. Save your insults for someone who'll appreciate them. You didn't find me despicable last night. Do I tell everyone you're my mistress and we're having a torrid affair, or do you tell them about us in a nice, polite manner?"

Abby's mouth dropped open. He pushed it shut with his finger then kissed her. Abby's towel fell when she reached up to put her arms around his neck. He blocked her from the view of anyone who might come in. While he kissed her, Judy came to tell Abby that breakfast was ready. She saw the kiss and walked out of the room.

"Abby?" Judy said from the doorway to her bedroom.

Reluctantly Abby pulled herself from Kyle's smoldering passion and put on her robe. Going to the door of her bath, she said, "Yes Mama?"

"Breakfast is ready."

"I'll be there in twenty minutes."

Abby hastily pushed Kyle from her room. "I have to get ready for work."

Twenty minutes later Abby was dressed in a white cashmere sweater and denim skirt. She had plaited her hair and brushed on her make-up with a light hand.

Hoping she had erased all signs of her passion filled night with Kyle, she pushed open the swinging door of the kitchen.

"Good morning." She said cheerily.

She was greeted by a chorus of good mornings. Andrew looked at his daughter. He smiled.

"What has you smiling this morning, Daddy?" Andrea asked.

"All my children under one roof." He lied easily.

"It has been a while since you were all home together." Judy joined in. "When K. M. Enterprises comes to Shelby we'll be together more often." Eric said.

"Speaking of which where is Kyle?" Abby asked casually.

"He went to town; said something about an errand he had to run." Eric told her.

"At this time of the morning?" Abby asked.

"That's what he said. I guess he wanted to get an early start looking for a building." Eric said.

"When will you be coming home?" Andrew asked.

"If everything goes right by the end of the year." Eric answered.

"By the end of the year? That long?" Abby questioned thoughtfully. She became lost in thought.

"Abby? Abby are you listening?" Eric's voice came to her.

"What? No, I wasn't listening. What did you say?" She asked.

"I said I didn't realize you missed me." Eric repeated.

"Yes, of course I do." She said absently.

Andrew watched Abby. She was troubled; he wasn't sure why, but he would bet anything her mind was on a blonde, blue-eyed man.

"Tabi you look tired. Didn't you sleep well last night?" He asked.

"Yes fine, Daddy." She answered.

Was she answering his question or making a generalized statement?

"You probably need a vacation." He pushed. "You've been looking peaked."

"Daddy what are you talking about? Abby looks fine." Andrea said puzzled.

"Don't you have to go to work Andrea?" Andrew asked pointedly.

Not understanding, Andrea stood up. Kissing both her parents, she put on her coat and left. Eric started to make a comment. Andrew shot him a dark look. Judy had been bustling around the kitchen while her family ate breakfast.

"Andrew shouldn't you be getting to the Pub? You did say a delivery was coming in this morning." She said tartly.

Startled at his wife's tone, Andrew looked at her. Her eyes told him if he didn't get out of there she wouldn't be responsible for what happened to him.

He kissed her good-bye then slammed out the door. His departure brought Abby from her musings. "What's wrong with Daddy?" She asked.

"Who knows? Probably woke up on the wrong side of the bed." Judy said.

"I've been away too long." Eric said, putting his dirty dishes in the sink.

He kissed his mother and sister then grabbed his coat and went to catch up with Kyle.

"What is Eric talking about, being away too long?" Abby asked.

"I don't know Dear." Judy told her.

Abby looked at her watch, she still had time before she had to leave for work.

"I'll help you with the dishes before I leave." She said.

"Abby are you all right?" Judy asked.

"Yes, fine. Why?"

"No reason, forget I asked. Do you know anything about the hot chocolate and Scotch I found on the counter this morning?"

"I couldn't sleep last night.I got up to make hot chocolate. Kyle came down to get a drink, I guess he couldn't sleep either."

Noticing the blush that had come into Abby's cheeks, Judy dropped the subject.

"Have you given anymore thought to attending the ball?"

"Not much. Why is it so important to Daddy that I attend?"

"Your father is worried about you. You haven't really dated since you broke your engagement."

"Mama I'm afraid to trust. I thought it would get easier but it hasn't."

"Of course not. Once it's broken, trust is hard to earn or give. Don't try so hard."

"Thanks Mama."

"For what?"

"Nothing... everything."

They finished the dishes. Impulsively Abby reached over to hug her mother.

Kyle walked in the back door. "Good morning." He said giving Abby a fiery smile.

She blushed, joining her mother in telling him good morning.

"Did Eric find you? I think he went to look for you." Abby told him.

"Yes, I met him outside a while ago. Were you on your way to work? Can I give you a ride?" Kyle said.

"Yes and no."

He arched a brow at her.

"Yes, I am on my way to work, and no I don't need a ride. Thanks, but I have a car."

"I'll walk you to your car." He said, taking her arm possessively.

She took her arm from his hold. "I have to get my purse and coat."

She told him. She went to get them. When she came back into the kitchen

Kyle and Judy ended the conversation they had been having. "Ready?" He asked.

She nodded and followed him out the door while she put on her coat. "What were you and Mama talking about?" Abby asked.

"Your birthday?" He suggested.

"Not until October, try again." She told him.

"The ball?" He hedged.

"Uh uh." She said.

"None of your business."

"You were talking about me."

"Quit fishing Sweetheart."

"Don't call me that."

"Don't call you what?"

"Sweetheart. I am not your Sweetheart."

"Querida?"

"Querida? What does it mean?"

"Mistress."

Her face went crimson. "Mistress? How do you know that?"

"I speak Spanish. You didn't answer my question."

"What question?"

"Would you like me to call you Querida?"

"Certainly not. Abby is fine."

"No, I think Querida suits you."

Looking away from him Abby glanced at her watch. She gave a small cry.

"I'm going to be late if I don't hurry."

"Don't forget about tonight."

"Tonight?"

"Telling your family we met in Atlanta."

She'd forgotten his threat. She opened her car door and stepped in. "I wasn't aware you had to use blackmail to get women into your bed." She slammed the door, started the engine and drove away.

# CHAPTER TWO

Kyle watched with menace as she drove away. His devilish smile promised retribution. His threat stayed with her all morning. She couldn't shake it. She wouldn't let him turn what they shared into something dirty and ugly. She had just finished typing the will that had been drafted that morning when her office door opened. Abby looked up as a teenage boy came in. "May I help you?" She asked.

"Are you Abby Phillips?" He asked. She nodded.

"These are for you." He said, handing her a vase wrapped in green florist's tissue, and then turned to leave.

"Wait." Abby said, bending to retrieve her purse from the bottom drawer of her desk.

"That's already been taken care of." He assured her and walked out. Tearing off the tissue, Abby gasped in surprise at the lovely roses. Twelve perfectly shaped peach roses. They hadn't yet opened to reveal their inner beauty. She looked for a card. Simply it read:

*Querida,*
*My Peach Rose, peach roses for the one whose virtue rests in my hands. I look forward to this evening's revelations as you look forward to the beauty these behold.*

*All my love, Kyle*

The nerve of the man! Who does he think he is? Remembering her parting shot to him that morning,

~ 33 ~

she shook. She was certain he wouldn't take her comment lightly.

Retribution for him would be swift if she'd read his face correctly. Telling her family they'd met in Atlanta was going to be a piece of cake compared to facing the devil incarnate. How dare he send her roses to remind her of his threat? For a moment she considered throwing his gift in the nearest trash. Reconsidering, she opted to leave them on her desk. Sitting them on a corner, she made short work of telling her boss she was going to lunch.

Abby was sitting in a café a few blocks from her office when Kyle and Eric walked in. She discreetly attracted their attention inviting them to join her.

"Hi, Mama said you'd be here for lunch." Eric told her when they sat down.

"What are you doing in town?" She asked.

"I'm searching for a building for the new K. M. Enterprises division." Kyle told her.

"Have you found anything?" Abby asked.

"Nothing I like." Kyle said irritably.

The waitress came to take their order. The next few minutes were spent ordering. Pretending to just have remembered something, Abby turned to Kyle. "Thank you for the roses, Kyle. They're lovely and it was sweet of you to send them after last night." She said.

His eyes were veiled when he looked at her. "I wasn't being sweet." He told her, a dangerous edge to his voice. She had been right when she'd thought of him as the devil incarnate. Eric eyed them speculatively.

"Did I miss something?"

Abby and Kyle responded simultaneously.

"No."

"Yes."

Eric laughed saying, "Well, which is it? Yes or no?"

Kyle was temporarily at a loss for words. Abby couldn't think of anything suitable to say so closed her mouth.

"Are you going to tell me, or is it a deep, dark secret?" Eric asked wickedly, raising his eyebrows lasciviously.

"All women should have flowers sent to them to remind them of their beauty." Kyle said.

"They did remind me of something." Abby admitted. "The night we met in Atlanta."

Kyle watched her from beneath half closed eyes. "You met Kyle in Atlanta?" Eric asked.

"Yes, I met him when I went to work for Aunt Millie." Abby stated.

"Why didn't you say something when I introduced you?" Eric questioned.

She refused to look in Kyle's direction. "It wasn't anything special, I didn't think it worth mentioning." She lied.

Kyle's eyes, calm and blue, had become dangerous points of steel-gray anger. Abby felt the inflexible control he kept on himself. Darting a glance in his direction, she was aware of deliberately provoking him.

There was a little devil inside her that wouldn't behave. She sensed that Kyle was near the boiling point. Before he could retaliate she skillfully changed the subject. Turning to him she said, "What made you decide to open a division of K. M. Enterprises in Shelby?"

Kyle's eyes narrowed until they became almost imperceptible gray slits. "Eric convinced me that Shelby would be a good place to open a new branch, as well as the size and location." He answered succinctly.

"You build computers?" She asked.

"Yes." Kyle said shortly.

"If my boss were to buy computers for the office how would K. M. Enterprises help?"

She was floundering and sensed he knew it.

"First, we'd work with him to decide what he wants them to do, help him choose the computer programs best suited to his needs. Second, we'd demonstrate how the computers could save him time and money. Last, we'd instruct him how to use them and the programs."

"I didn't know you were interested in computers, Abby." Eric said.

"I've been trying to convince my boss to buy computers for the office. If I can get an expert to talk to him he may consider buying them."

For the remainder of the lunch hour Abby neatly avoided any conversation about her and Kyle meeting in Atlanta. The afternoon sped by as she typed the letters her boss had dictated. She expected Kyle to take revenge after what she'd done at lunch and for her comment that morning. She jumped when the phone rang. Her heart jumped into her throat whenever her office door opened. He did nothing by word or deed. She was relieved, yet afraid. The waiting was torture. When the grandfather clock pealed at five, Abby couldn't have been gladder. She raced home. She changed from her sweater and skirt into faded jeans and one of Eric's old jerseys.

"The best way to get through the evening is to act as though our previous acquaintance wasn't anything special. Say it enough and you'll almost believe it yourself." She said silently going down the stairs. Andrew noticed her come into the room first. "So Tabi, you met Kyle in Atlanta." He said.

"Yes Daddy, I met Kyle in Atlanta." She admitted reluctantly. Abby dreaded the interrogation she knew was coming.

She could feel Kyle's eyes on her. Like a magnet hers were irresistibly drawn to his. They drew battle lines, warring against one another.

His eyes told her "Revenge is sweet." He knew waiting for him to avenge himself was torture. He smiled.

Abby broke eye contact first. She could see that Andrew wanted to inquire more on the subject of their first meeting. Judy came in to announce supper. All went into the dining room.

"It's so romantic. Lovers meet by chance are torn apart by fate then brought back together by circumstance." Andrea sighed.

Abby tensed, her eyes flew to Andrea. Seeing only that her sister had poorly chosen her words, she relaxed. Kyle felt Abby tense then relax.

He saw the look of apology Andrea sent her.

"Don't be ridiculous, Andie." Abby said.

"Love works mysteriously, Abby. Don't be so quick to laugh." Judy scolded.

"I'm sorry, Mama. The way Andie said it makes it sound ridiculous." Abby apologized.

Kyle was again at Abby's right, caressing her inner thigh. Seeming not to notice his action, he became attentive toward Andrea. Anger and jealousy at Kyle surged through Abby. He felt the emotions running through her, pretending to wonder what caused them.

"Why do you call Abby, Tabi?" Kyle asked Andrew.

Andrew laughed. "Her name is Tabitha, after my mother. I've always called her Tabi. When she was born she sounded like a mad kitten, therefore I thought of Mama, and gave her the name." Andrew said.

"No one else uses the stupid nickname." Abby warned, directing a nasty look at her father.

"I'll tell you more about it another time." Andrew promised.

"Not if I can help it." Abby muttered.

"Why didn't you tell us you'd met Kyle while you were working for Millie?" Andrew asked her.

Abby knew the questions would come. She repeated the same lies she'd told Eric at lunch. Only Andrea noticed the barely perceptible anger Kyle held in check.

"Abby can I see you in the kitchen?" She asked.

Grateful to escape her family's inquisition, Abby excused herself. Andrea rounded on her, emerald eyes flashing, when she walked into the kitchen.

"Why are you telling those lies?" Andrea spat.

Abby stepped back. "Am I supposed to tell Daddy I slept with the man shortly after I met him?" She shot back

"I didn't say that." Andie said.

"Then mind your own business." Abby told her. She walked out of the kitchen, back into the dining room.

After supper she volunteered to clean up, waving aside Judy's protests. "Relax, ask Daddy to take you for a stroll in the meadow." Abby insisted.

"We haven't taken a walk in the snow for years. A lovely way to end the day." Judy agreed. She went to get her coat and drag Andrew out for a walk. Eric and Andrea were going out for the evening. Abby and Kyle were left alone in the house.

"I'll help clean up." He told her walking into the kitchen.

"It isn't necessary, you are a guest." She reminded him.

"I'd like to talk to you. I might as well help while we talk." He said.

She shrugged saying, "Suit yourself."

They cleaned up in strained silence. Kyle decided to wait until after they'd cleaned up to talk to her. Abby pulled away sharply when they accidentally touched.

"You don't have to pull away from me." Kyle snarled.

"I'm not pulling away from you." She said tartly.

He let the lie go.

Abby made a fresh pot of coffee.

"Would you like some coffee?" She asked.

"I'd like more than coffee but that will do for a start." He said.

"Cream and sugar?" She asked while she set up a serving tray.

"Damn it, Abby, stop treating me like a stranger." He barked.

"How would you like me to treat you? We've been lovers yet I know nothing about you."

"At least you admit we've been lovers. Why did you lie to your family about our relationship?"

"I don't want to discuss this Kyle."

Annoyed, he wanted to shake her; instead he changed tactics. "What would you like to know about me?"

"Nothing, everything, I want to forget what I do know about you. I don't know what I want."

She fought with the emotions while looking around the kitchen for something to occupy herself. There wasn't anything. Noting her confusion, Kyle pushed her to continue. "Tell me Abby."

"Tell you what?" She asked.

"You know damn well what." He snarled.

"You do things to me that I can't explain. You make me feel things I don't want to feel. I don't want to fall in love with you." She told him. She turned away from him. He turned her around to face him.

The tears started to fall; once started they couldn't be stopped. He held her as she cried. The hurt and anger she'd held in, after her initial reaction to Richard and Jessie's betrayal, came flooding out. When her crying subsided she stepped away from him.

"I went to Aunt Millie's to get away from the pity and sympathy after I broke my engagement." She told him.

"I'm a good listener, Querida. Tell me about your lost love." He said, fearing she wasn't over her former fiancée.

"There is no lost love." She said sarcastically. Abby went to watch the sunset.

"Tell me about your engagement." He said gently. "I'd rather not go into that relationship Kyle."

"Something about it has made you afraid to get involved with me. Tell me about it Abby."

"Kyle, I told you..."

He walked up behind her. She knew he was there. He turned her to face him and looked into her chocolate brown eyes.

"I know what you told me, now tell me what I want to know." His tone challenged her to argue.

"All right, but remember I warned you."

He nodded.

"When he first asked me out I was a freshman, he was a senior. I was thrilled, the other girls were jealous. All of them had tried to catch his eye."

"Some went as far as to further their acquaintance with me to be near him. I had many friends. I trusted Jessie most, we had been friends forever."

The coffee maker stopped. Ignoring the serving tray Kyle poured coffee for both of them. Abby accepted the cup he held out to her and added milk to hers, then took a drink; he drank his black.

"We had been dating for three and a half years when he proposed. He took me to supper on Valentine's Day, proposing after we'd eaten."

He said, "Our relationship means a lot to me."

"His need for a wife and eventually children were essential to his career. His wife would be hostess at the dinner parties he would give for his father's clients and associates."

"What about love, Querida?" Kyle interrupted.

She laughed scornfully. "I thought it went without saying. I told him I loved him often. He told me he loved me whenever he wanted to get me into bed."

Involuntarily Kyle's hands made fists at the thought of any man, except himself, who tried to get his woman into bed.

"He wanted me to graduate before I became 'an old married woman.' His family was happy when we announced our engagement. My family wasn't. Jessie wasn't happy at the announcement either. I believed her to be upset at the possibility of losing our friendship. I assured her often that her friendship meant as much to me as he did."

"Why didn't your family approve?" Kyle asked.

"How did you know my family didn't approve?" She asked.

"Wild guess, go on." He told her.

"I asked Jessie to be a bridesmaid in the wedding. Andrea was going to be my maid of honor. As I prepared for graduation Mama and Mrs. Dalton planned our wedding. It was going to be the most beautiful wedding this town had ever seen."

Abby took a drink of her coffee, finding it had cooled she went to pour more. Offering more to Kyle, she put it back at his negative response.

"While I was walking on air my best friend and fiancée were sleeping together. I had heard rumors about Jessie but hadn't believed them. I was later told they had been sleeping together since the beginning of our junior year."

"On my last day of classes I was overjoyed. I went to his apartment to make supper for him."

Becoming restless Abby took out ingredients for chocolate chip cookies. She measured them into a bowl and stirred them. Kyle watched as she did busy work. He went to hold her; she stepped out of his embrace.

"I heard noises in the bedroom. I went to see what it was. Imagine my surprise when I found my fiancée and best friend in bed together. I was so embarrassed at having walked in on them in bed, all I could do was let out a small cry and turn away."

Richard heard me. He said, "It isn't as bad as it looks." Putting the bowl of dough aside, Abby preheated the oven.

"At that point I turned around. I took his ring off, threw it at him then put his apartment key on his dresser. Calling Richard an obscene name I told Jessie I hadn't believed the rumors being spread about her and ran out of the apartment." Abby finished. She'd told him her story without emotion.

"You then went to your aunt's in Atlanta." Kyle stated.

"No, a few days before my aborted wedding day." Abby corrected.

"You haven't discussed it with either of them." He said.

"No, Shelby is big enough that I didn't have to unless I chose to. I chose not to, I didn't want to hear their pathetic lies." She told him.

"You haven't spoken to either of them since until I refused to let you run away from her last night?"

"I wasn't trying to run away. If you hadn't interfered I could have gone on with my life as I had before."

"Gone on with your life? What kind of life did you have?"

"My life was just fine until you came back into it. You turned my world upside down once. It took me years to turn it back. I will not let you do it again."

He stood staring at her in stony silence.

She turned away. He broke the silence bringing up a more sensitive subject. "What about a husband and children, a home of your own?"

"I don't want or need a husband. Maybe someday I'll have children and a home of my own. Now if you'll excuse me I'd like to finish my cookies."

"Children without a husband, how would your family accept that bit of news? You're running away again, Querida. I thought you had more courage."

Abby turned to him; she wasn't given a chance to answer. Judy and Andrew walked into the kitchen.

"Have you remembered your manners to our guest?" Andrew asked feeling the tension vibrate through the room.

"Your daughter's manners are flawless." Kyle assured him. Andrew looked from one to the other. Sparks were flying.

"Would anyone like coffee?" Judy asked to ease the tension.

"I'll get it Mama." Abby told her. "I was just making cookies."

"Chocolate chip I assume." Andrew said hopefully.

"Are there any other kind?" Abby asked playfully, pouring coffee. She'd put dough onto a pan. Now she put it into the oven.

"Andrew, you promised to tell me more about Abby's name." Kyle reminded him.

Abby turned to glare at Kyle. Looking at her father she warned him not to say anything. Both ignored her.

"Mama despised nicknames. She insisted everyone call her Tabitha. One day Papa was at Mama's house visiting her older brother. He started teasing her; she got so mad she started hissing like an angry cat. He told her she sounded like a tabby cat. After that he called her Tabi. She threatened to thrash anyone who dared call her granddaughter by the ridiculous nickname." Andrew told him.

"How did you escape her thrashing?" Kyle asked.

"Simple. I told Mama I'd named my daughter after her because she reminded me of my dear, sweet mama." Andrew told him proudly.

Kyle chuckled. Abby groaned. She scowled at him while she took the cookies out of the oven and put more in.

"Why is she called Abby?" Kyle asked.

"We shortened Tabi." Andrew said.

"I'd like to meet your mother. Does Abby take after her?" Kyle asked.

"In some ways yes, she is like Mama." Andrew answered.

Abby's hand jerked as she put more dough onto the cookie sheet when Kyle had asked about her grandmother.

"Nana Phillips passed away seven years ago Kyle." Abby told him gently.

Andrew watched Kyle study Abby. He saw the softness come into his eyes when Abby told him of the loss of her beloved grandmother.

"I'm sorry Abby. I didn't mean to upset you." Kyle apologized.

"No harm done." Abby told him.

"That reminds me Andrew, Papa Phillips is coming over tomorrow." Judy said.

"Did he say why?" Andrew asked.

"Only that he's heard talk in town about Abby's new beau. He said something about the Goodson girl spreading a rumor." Judy said.

"My new beau, that's ridiculous I don't have a new beau. Jessie never could keep her mouth shut." Abby snapped.

"Tabitha!" Andrew said sharply.

The shock of her father using her given name got Abby's attention. She stared at him; he stared back for a moment. His eyes warned her.

Dawning comprehension took root in her brain.

"Good Lord you don't think...granddaddy doesn't think..."

"That's exactly what I think, so, I assume does Papa." Andrew warned audibly.

Abby looked noisily under the cupboard for another cookie sheet. She didn't find one just as she knew she wouldn't.

"Here Daddy have a cookie." She said glaring and shoving a cookie at him. Turning to Kyle, "Can I get you more coffee?"

He smiled, enjoying watching her get flustered. "No thanks.  I will have a cookie though."

Abby took the second pan out of the oven. Setting it in front of him on the table she said, "Enjoy."

Going to the counter she took the batch there and put it into the oven. Kyle bit into his cookie. "Mm mm.  These are the best chocolate chip cookies I've ever tasted. My mother always tells me 'if you find a woman who can cook you ought to marry her'." He told her.

"I'm sure your mother didn't mean for you to take her literally." Abby said.

"I think mother says it because I refused to learn to cook.  When I moved out and into a hotel with a small kitchen I wished I had listened to her. My cooking was terrible."

A thought occurred to him.

"Abby when I find a house in Shelby would you be willing to take care of it for me?"

Abby's movements became spasmodic at Kyle's joke.

Kyle and Andrew smiled. Judy elbowed Andrew in the ribs. He quit smiling.

Abby had her back to them; they couldn't see her open and close her mouth, only to open it again.

"What's the matter Tabi? Cat got your tongue?" Andrew teased.

"No, cat hasn't got my tongue. I don't think Kyle's little joke is funny. If I'm going to take care of any man's house he'll be my husband." Abby stated.

She walked to the table and picked up a cookie, taking a bite. Kyle took her hand putting the remainder into his mouth. After he'd eaten it he suckled her fingers. Slowly he released her tingling fingers and gazed into her liquid brown eyes.

Slowly she backed away from him, still within easy reach. He easily caught her wrist tumbling her into his lap. Once there, he settled her comfortably kissing her.

Drowning in his possession she entirely forgot her parents' presence. For her the kiss ended all too soon. Kyle's eyes were like a gentle ocean when he brought her softly back to reality.

As the kiss ended Andrew cleared his throat to remind them they were not alone.

"I do believe Mrs. Phillips we have just witnessed the best example of sampling cookies that I've ever seen." Andrew teased.

Abby drew herself off of Kyle's lap. She went to the oven to remove the cookies then put the next batch in. Placing the pan on the counter, she removed the cookies to set them on the cooling rack. Judy went to stand next to her. "Don't pay your Daddy any mind it's been so long since you've been interested in a boy." She whispered softly.

"Kyle is hardly a boy Mama, he's thirty-three. I'm twenty-three, I think I can handle a little teasing." Abby whispered back.

"Kyle has shown a great deal of interest in you child. Don't let the past get in the way of a relationship between you." Judy murmured.

"What are you two cooking up now?" Andrew asked suspiciously.

"I told you I was making cookies Daddy." Abby answered flippantly. She took the cookies from the oven and put another batch in.

"Watch these women, son. Before you know it they'll have you doing things you had no intention doing." Andrew cautioned.

Turning to her father, Abby asked, "Have you always been so suspicious of women Daddy?"

"It's a sure sign of trouble when they whisper." Andrew said.

Kyle chuckled at the lighthearted banter between father and daughter. "Most trouble begins at the hands of a woman." He said.

Abby's mouth dropped open.

"It's a beautiful night for a walk." Kyle said. He walked to Abby, grasped her hand, and virtually dragged her out the door taking their coats off the hooks.

"Thank you Kyle, I'd love to take a walk with you." Abby said tartly.

"We'll finish the cookies for you." Andrew said helpfully as they walked out the door.

When they were out of earshot of the house she said, "Why did you do that?"

"Do what?" He asked.

"Nearly make love to me in the kitchen then drag me out of the house." She snapped.

"I warned you about our relationship. I want you Querida. When Andrew discovers we became lovers the night we met I won't deny it." He told her.

He pulled her to him gently pressing his lips to hers. Abby allowed him to use his hands and mouth to arouse her until images of his behavior at supper began to swim before her. She pushed him away from her, her hands on his chest.

"No Kyle, I will not allow you to make love to me after your behavior tonight. I will not compete with Andrea." She stated.

"You've lost me Querida. What are you talking about?" He said harshly.

"You were pawing me during supper and your attentiveness toward Andrea. At least Richard was clever enough to keep his affair a secret from me."

Kyle let her go. "Don't compare me with that fool. You're jealous!"

"No Kyle, I'm not jealous. I will not be jealous because of a man." She lied. "Don't use me to satisfy your desires and don't use Andie as bait. I've had enough of faithless males to last a lifetime."

"I've never in my life used anyone. I've been faithful to..." Kyle broke off. He had been mentally faithful to her. For nearly five years he had dreamed of the raven-haired beauty who had imbedded herself into his heart.

"Are you asking me to be faithful to you Querida?"

He took her by the shoulders and forced her to look at him.

"No! I don't care if you have a dozen affairs. Don't expect me to be one of them."

"Marry me."

Her brown eyes locked with his colorless gaze. He was serious.

"Are you out of your mind? We can't get married."

"Why not?"

"I don't want a husband, remember. Besides I won't marry a man who doesn't love me."

He'd been stupid trying to make her jealous. Mentally kicking himself he turned and walked away from her.

"Are you ashamed that we've been lovers Querida?" He asked lightly, changing the subject.

"Not ashamed exactly..." She stopped, trying to find the words to explain.

He didn't wait for her to finish.  "You'd rather no one know we've been lovers." He stated caustically. Kyle turned around to face her.  There was fear in her eyes.  Or was there?

"The fewer people who know the less chance..."

"The less chance what?"

She looked at him in careful silence pleading with him to understand.

"I won't play your games and I won't be kept a secret because some fool once broke your heart. Damn it Abby, I'm not Richard."

"No you're more dangerous. You can do something he never could."

"What can't that fool do that you're so afraid of?"

"Nothing, I'm not afraid of him."

Walking back to her he shook her. "What are you afraid of Abby? Tell me why you won't give us a chance." Kyle pleaded.

"You'll break my heart. You've already proven you can't be trusted." She told him.

"I can't be..." Realizing she wasn't going to believe anything he said, Kyle stopped. "I understand your need to trust. Give us a chance."

Breaking free of his hold she turned her back to him. "I can't. I'm going for a drive. Tell Mama not to wait up." She said, unaware of the tremor in her voice.

"You can't or you won't?" He said to her back. She pretended not to hear.

"Damn it to hell! He'd never come across as bothersome a female as Tabitha Phillips. She's my woman. I'm going to brand her like cowboys brand their cattle. It's just a matter of how."

Kyle strode to the house determined to make Abby admit she didn't want him to leave her alone. Abby climbed into her car and rested her head on the steering wheel. She took huge gulps of air to get her breathing under control. Sitting there for a long time she brought herself under control. Starting the car she drove around Shelby thinking over the years since she'd broken her engagement.

"Daddy and Andrea are right I have to get on with my life. I let Jessie and Richard steal nearly five years I won't let them have another second. I'm going to the Spring Ball." She told herself sternly.

Abby drove back to the house. Parking her car, she noticed a light on in the kitchen. She'd asked Kyle to tell Mama not to wait up. Fumbling for her keys to unlock the door, she jumped back nearly falling off the porch when Kyle flung the door open.

"Well it's about time. Where have you been? I've been waiting for you." He said.

Abby stood dazed running her eyes over him. He didn't have anything on. Well he might as well not have had anything on. He was only wearing briefs and there wasn't much to them. He took her hand pulling her into the house. "I don't like waiting, it takes up too much time." He said then kissed her.

He'd seen the way she had looked him over. Now they were getting somewhere. It was going to kill him but he had to go through with his plan if he expected her to move to Atlanta...permanently.

Andrew came running down the stairs when he heard the door slam against the wall. He ran into the kitchen, stopping when he saw Kyle kissing his daughter.

He saw where the knob had hit the wall and left a hole. It could easily be repaired. Kyle let Abby up for air. She saw her father and blushed. Kyle saw the blush and turned around to find the source.

"I heard the door and came to check...I see you have everything under control. I'll see you in the morning, good night." Andrew said to Kyle hurriedly leaving the room smiling.

Before Abby could gather her senses Kyle pulled her to him again. Her head was spinning she couldn't get her bearings. Kyle was going to make love to her.

She tried to think rationally but her senses had gone on vacation. He was kissing her mouth then taking little nips at her neck.

His hands were molding her to him but their bodies weren't touching.

"Kyle please, I'm on fire."

At her pleading he almost lost control. He suckled, nipped, kissed and touched. He could feel the heat he was creating. He picked her up and carried her up the stairs. After closing the door to her bedroom he laid Abby on her bed, undressing them both.

"Kyle this is torture, love me."

"I'll make love to you when the time is right Querida."

Kyle's hands roamed over her body slowly torturing. Abby arched into them when they found her most intimate part. He withdrew and replaced his hands with his mouth. He traveled the same path with his mouth as his hands. She arched and bucked pulling her to him. He lost control. He pulled away from her then. Abby stiffened.

"I'm sorry, Love." He whispered.

He held her, easing the painful pleasure as spasms rocked her body. Short gasps broke free as her release came. He knew the moment she lost consciousness. Her whispered "I love you Kyle," was the last thing she'd said. He held her close. He would never forget the whispered words, but she wouldn't remember them in the morning. Tears formed in his eyes. She could say the words in passion but she wouldn't say them in the cold light of day. He listened to her sleep. Her breathing was even. He slipped out of her bed and drew on his briefs. She was going to hate them both in the morning, herself most. He'd only meant to tease, hoping she'd come to him on her own. Damn! He'd lost control and very possibly the only woman he'd ever love. Kyle walked down the hall to his own room.

# CHAPTER THREE

The tears Abby had shed before telling Kyle about her broken engagement had released the pain and anger that she had bottled up for so long. She climbed out of bed to shower and dress. While she went down to breakfast her heart sang a happy tune. She was in love and nothing could be as wonderful. In love! She was shocked! How could she have fallen in love? This wasn't supposed to happen. The realization that she was in love with Kyle was painful. He'd wanted her last night but hadn't said anything about loving her. Determined to ignore her foolish heart, she pinned a smile on her face and went into the kitchen.

"Good morning, Mama, Daddy. Good morning everyone. Isn't it a lovely day?" She said cheerfully, going to sit in her usual spot next to Kyle.

"You're in a better mood this morning." Kyle said. Her heart beat a little faster than normal.

"What has you in a cheery mood this morning? Andrew asked. It's either of two things: you're in love or you're up to something."

Kyle looked expectantly at Abby. She gave nothing away.

"Can't I simply be in a cheery mood without you becoming suspicious?" Abby asked.

"I suppose it is possible, but I still think you're up to something." Andrew stated.

"If you must know, I've decided to go to the Spring Ball." She announced.

"I'm delighted you've changed your mind." Andrew said as he drew away from the table. "I'll be in my study."

He walked out of the room. Andrea went off like a machine gun. "What changed your mind? After all you were dead set against going."

"I decided you and Daddy are right. I have been hiding from the world. I'm going to stop running away from life and live it." Abby said staring pointedly at Kyle. He acknowledged the rebuke with a nod of his head.

"Are you taking Jessie to the Spring Ball, Eric?" Andrea asked.

"Yes why?" Eric answered.

"Abby doesn't have a date." Andrea pointed out.

"Don't worry about me. It's not unusual for a lady to go unescorted." Abby told her.

"I'd be honored to escort you Abby." Kyle volunteered.

"I didn't know you were going to be here for the ball." Abby answered.

"I hadn't intended to be. I made my decision to go last night as well. Going to the ball will enable me to meet some of the people in town. Having a beautiful woman on my arm will be icing on the cake." He said, only half lying.

"Having you as an escort will be an honor kind sir." She said serenely. "Who are you going with Andie?"

Andrea looked sheepish. "Richard asked me weeks ago." Andrea hedged.

"That doesn't answer my question. Did you accept his invitation?" Abby drew out the last question. Slowly Andrea drew her emerald gaze away from her sister. "Of course not, I think he only asked me to make you jealous." She replied petulantly.

"For heaven's sake why are you so angry? I only asked who your date is. He can't be that bad. Who is he?" Abby asked sharply.

"Anthony Caldoni!" Andrea snapped.

Abby opened her mouth to respond, and then snapped it shut. Kyle was kneading the inside of her thigh. She waited a moment then said, "There's no need to snap at me, Andie. I simply asked who your date is."

"Tabitha! We do have a guest." Judy scolded.

"I apologize for my lack of manners, Kyle." She said.

Kyle accepted her apology, nodding his head. Abby stood. "If you'll excuse me, I have errands to run." She said.

Leaving the dining room, she almost collided with her grandfather. "Good morning Tabitha." He greeted her.

"Good morning Granddaddy." She greeted rushing past him to get her coat.

"Judy, what has my granddaughter in a snit this morning?" Samuel Phillips demanded.

Judy walked to her father-in-law to kiss his cheek.

"Just a little misunderstanding Papa." Judy told him after kissing him.

Ignoring the others in the room he said, "It sounds interesting, I don't have time to get into it now. I need to talk to Andrew, where is he?"

"In the study, shall I get him?" Judy asked.

"No, I'll go to the study. I'd like to speak to him alone." He said.

Driving into town, Abby saw her hometown, as she hadn't before. The people were friendly and took strangers into their midst comfortably. They only need to pass through to be welcomed.

She had spent her life in this small community. Never going very far, except on occasion to Aunt Millie's in Atlanta. She was well loved and respected.

Her brown eyes looked at the familiar buildings as her long, black hair blew around her face from the partially open window. Pushing it back, she reached into her purse for the elastic bands she always carried. Stopping in front of the post office, she loosely plaited her hair. Stepping out of her car, Abby pulled her coat closer around her. She walked into the building and was greeted by the postmistress.

"Good morning, Abby. What brings you out on a day like this?" Wendy asked.

"Good morning, Wendy. I wanted to get out of the house." Abby told her.

"Why did you want to get out of the house? According to Jessie, there's a gorgeous man staying at your house." Wendy stated.

"Jessie thinks any man who seems affluent is gorgeous." Abby responded waspishly.

Looking at her friend in surprise, Wendy said, "Still haven't made-up with her I see. I don't blame you but don't let your anger get the best of you."

"It'll be a cold day in hell when I make-up with her. I'm not angry anymore, I'll never trust her again." Abby told her.

"I'm just looking to confirm what Jessie is spreading around town. She says the man has shown a great deal of interest in you." Wendy warned.

"Jessie has a wild imagination. Can I have two books of stamps please?" Abby quickly changed the subject.

Puzzled at her friend's rudeness, Wendy gave Abby the stamps, taking the money she held out and handed her the change.

"You'll meet Kyle at the Spring Ball, he's my escort." Abby said as she walked out. Smiling to herself, Abby nearly walked into Richard Dalton. She instinctively stepped away from his steadying grip.

"Don't touch me." She hissed.

"Well, well if it isn't Abby Phillips. How long has it been?" He snarled.

"Not long enough! I have things to do!" She snapped.

He blocked her path when she tried to walk around him. "I want to talk to you." He commanded.

"We have nothing to talk about." She answered.

"I wanted to explain...do you hate me so much that you're willing to throw away what we had together? I still love you and I always will." He said.

"I don't hate you, Richard. I would have to feel something for you if I did. I don't. As for loving me, you love what I was nearly five years ago. I'm no longer the innocent child you wanted to marry." She told him.

"You're still the only woman for me Abby. I'll make you come around. You love me, you're just too stubborn to admit it." He promised.

"I don't love you, Richard. Do yourself a favor and forget about me." Abby said.

Richard saw movement behind Abby. She was roughly hauled against a wide, muscular chest.

"You promised you wouldn't go wandering around without me, Querida. And here I find you with another man." Kyle accused.

"Take your hands off my fiancée." Richard demanded.

"Fiancée, you didn't tell me you were engaged, Querida." Kyle said, looking down at Abby, his tone a warning to Richard.

Abby's breath came out in a rush. "Kyle."She caught her breath. "I'm not. He must have me confused with someone else."

She'd never been so glad to see anyone in her life. Kyle pulled her closer.

"Of course it's me, Querida. You didn't think I'd abandoned you just because we've had a lovers' quarrel." He said seductively.

"No Darling, I was upset with you, I thought shopping would cheer me up." She answered, turning in his arms. His hands cupped her bottom and pulled her closer for his kiss. Moments later Kyle released her.

"Am I forgiven?" He asked in the same seductive voice.

"Forgiven for what?"

He smiled down at her. "Nothing, aren't you going to introduce me to your friend?"

Abby had forgotten Richard. She turned around. Kyle wrapped his arms around her in a lover's caress.

"Kyle Masterson, Richard Dalton." She said.

Kyle stiffened. He didn't warn Richard how close he had come to punching him when he'd seen him accost Abby. He stuck out his hand. Warily, Richard gave him a loose grip and visibly winced at the finger-crushing grip Kyle gave him. Returning his attention to Abby, Kyle said, "Do you still have more shopping to do or can I take you home now?"

He bent to whisper in her ear, causing Abby to blush to the roots of her hair. He pulled her along.

"Damn it, Abby. I wanted to talk to you." Richard whined.

"No time. She has to take care of me." Kyle threw over his shoulder. Walking to the grocery, Abby fought the urge to laugh.

"Thanks for rescuing me. I didn't know how I was going to get out of talking to him." She told Kyle.

"Don't thank me. I was only doing what any lover would do, protecting my interests from predators like him." Kyle told her.

"Now wait just a damn minute." She said stopping.

"No, I don't want you to see him again." He told her, taking her arm in a firm grip to hurry her along.

"I appreciate your help back there, but I will not take orders from you. I'll see who I want."

"Not if I have anything to say about it." He said, pulling her toward him to kiss away her defiance. Lifting his head, he said, "Where are your car keys? Eric dropped me off."

She handed him her keys.

"Where is your car?"

"Over at the post office." She started to give him directions, but he waved them off.

"I'll meet you there in half an hour." He strode away.

Abby walked to the grocery. Entering, she was greeted by Jasmine. "Was that the man Jessie has been telling the whole town about?" She asked tactlessly.

"Yes, he's Eric's boss." Abby answered, her face going crimson.

"Just Eric's boss?" Jasmine asked curiously.

"Jessie has made darn sure everyone knows there may be a new man in my life." Abby commented, changing the subject.

The effort was wasted on Jasmine.

"It's not every day a man like that comes to town." Jasmine blurted. "No, but when K. M. Enterprises comes to Shelby, there will be enough men for all of the women to have their pick. Jessie will drop Eric like a hot potato to snare someone higher on the corporate ladder." Abby said angrily.

"Jessie is dating Eric?" Jasmine asked shocked.

"She is." Abby stated flatly.

"Why? Eric isn't the type she usually goes out with." Jasmine said.

"Eric is ambitious, but he could learn a few tricks from her. I only hope he doesn't get hurt in the process. She'll dump him as soon as she realizes there are bigger fish to fry." Abby agreed.

"I suppose neither of you has ever heard of true love." Jessie replied from the doorway, tears in her eyes.

"Where you're concerned? Hardly." Abby said.

"How can I make you understand that what I did, I did to keep you from being hurt?" She begged.

"I'll never understand, Jessie. It had been going on for nearly two years." Turning to Jasmine, "I have a few things to get, I'll look around until she's gone."

After leaving the store, Abby went to her car. Kyle was waiting. He leaned across the seat to brush her lips with his. "Do you need anything else?" He asked, lifting his head.

"No, we can go home." Abby said, huskiness in her voice.

He drove them back to the house. Along the way she enjoyed the falling snow and the beauty it brought. When they pulled into the drive she thought about what she would need for the ball. First she'd have to see the gown her mother had made. Gathering her purchases, Abby and Kyle went into the house. Judy was in the kitchen making lunch. Looking up when they came in, she said, "I kept your breakfast warm if you want it."

"How long until lunch?" Abby asked, setting down her packages.

"About an hour." Judy said.

"I'll wait for lunch." Kyle and Abby said together.

"Afterwards I'd like to look at my ball gown. I want to get an idea of what accessories I'll need." Abby said.

"You'll need slippers, a petticoat, a handbag and you can wear my pearl earrings." Judy told her.

"I'll have to go back to town this afternoon."

"I'll give you a piece of material to take with you, that way you'll be able to match the color."

After lunch Judy and Abby excused themselves to look at her gown. Abby put it on. While watching her daughter, tears formed in Judy's eyes. "You look lovely, Abby. The gown sets off your creamy skin and dark hair perfectly." She declared.

Abby turned to look at herself in the mirror. She was astonished. "Is that really me?" She asked, peering closer to see her reflection better.

"Don't be so surprised, dear. You're only now seeing what others have always seen." Judy told her.

Abby stared at her reflection. "I've always dreamed of being as beautiful as this, but never thought it possible." She admitted.

"Not possible? How could it not be possible when you look like me?" Andrea asked, walking into the room.

Abby turned to look at her sister. "With your blonde hair and dark skin you command attention wherever you go." Abby sighed.

"Is something wrong with your eyes? Haven't you ever noticed the way men look at you? If looks could talk... let's just say they'd say hot with a capital H. I've often wished I had your dark hair and creamy skin." Andrea confessed.

"Enough of this. You're both beautiful in your own way. Andrea, try on your gown." Judy said.

Andrea put on her gown. To her amazement, she saw in herself what she had always seen in her sister.

"At the ball, no man alive will escape heart palpitations after they see the two of us." Andrea said without conceit.

Abby and Andrea giggled.

Abby saw tears form in her mother's eyes for the second time that day.

"What's wrong, Mama? Is something bothering you?" She asked thoughtfully.

Judy wiped her eyes. "I can't believe you're grown up already. It seems like I was holding you in my arms yesterday. Now you're ready to start families of your own."

"You'll have to settle for Eric and Andrea having families. I'm not getting married." Abby stated blankly.

"But I thought you and Kyle..." Judy started to say.

"There is nothing between us. I'm just a pleasant diversion for him while he's in town." Abby said.

"He acts as though..." Judy said.

"He's very good at pretense, Mama. Now, can we work on our gowns? I'd rather not discuss my love life, or lack of." Abby told them. They made the adjustments to alter their gowns.

Abby and Andrea went into town to pick up accessories. While they were there they ran into Jessie.

"Shopping for your Mama, Abby?" Jessie asked caustically.

Sugar sweet, Abby replied, "No, I'm going to enter the Spring Ball Queen Pageant. These are for me."

"That color hardly suits you. You should wear something darker to set off your fair complexion." Jessie said tartly.

"Oh this color suits me as well as scarlet suits you. Let's go Andie." Abby urged.

"Did you see her face? She turned five shades of red. Abby, what's gotten into you?" Andrea snickered.

"I told you I was going to live life again. That includes showing the likes of her I won't stay down when I'm pushed." Abby answered.

"Remind me never to cross you. I wouldn't want you for an enemy." Andrea said.

They finished their shopping and then headed home. When they arrived Samuel was in the kitchen with Judy.

"How was your shopping trip?" He asked.

"You should have been there Granddaddy! We ran into Jessie she was being catty, Abby called her a scarlet woman." Andrea told them.

"Tabitha, you didn't!" Judy said shocked.

Abby though for a moment, then smiled. "I guess I did." She admitted.

"I wouldn't be so proud of myself young lady. You deliberately hurt Jessie." Judy scolded.

"Now Judy, you don't know what happened. Don't scold Tabitha until you've learned the facts." Samuel said.

"What happened today, Abby?" Judy questioned.

Abby refused to answer. Andrea related the afternoon's events.

"What do you expect Tabitha to do? Let the girl insult her and walk away." Samuel demanded.

"Of course not, but she should be more discreet." Judy answered.

"I won't let her nasty comments upset me and I won't walk away from her insults."

Abby turned and walked out of the room. Kyle and Eric went back to Atlanta the following week. Abby and her family prepared for the ball and helped the residents of Shelby decorate the town. As the day of the ball drew near, Shelby became a show place of life renewing itself. She put in her entry to compete in the Spring Ball pageant and was told she could compete in the Senior Miss Division. The committee asked her to crown the winner of the Junior Miss Division. Abby worried that Kyle wouldn't be back in time for the ball. She thought about him often. Finally the day of the ball arrived. Eric left to pick up Jessie.

"Mama I can't find my slippers." Andrea cried.

"Mama I can't find the earrings you promised me." Abby cried.

"I can't be in two places at once." Judy stated calmly.

Appearing in Andrea's doorway, she said, "Did you clean your contacts this morning, Andrea? Your slippers are on your bed."

Going to Abby's room, she asked, "Abby do you have your contacts in? "Of course not, that's your jewelry box, not mine."

"If women kept themselves organized it wouldn't take them so long to dress." Samuel grumbled.

"And they wouldn't keep us waiting." Andrew joined in.

"That's a fine way to talk after all the trouble we go through to make ourselves beautiful for you." Judy said walking to her husband.

"My Darling if these are the results of my wait I won't complain again." Andrew declared looking at her.

"I should hope not." Judy said.

"Where are my granddaughters?" Samuel demanded.

Everyone turned their heads when they heard a rustle come from the top of the stairs. Andrea stood at the top of the stairs. Dressed in a pale green gown, with a v-neck, she descended the stairs. Peeking from beneath her gown were slippers an exact match to her gown and her handbag was lost to the background of it. Her hair was twisted into a knot at the back of her head with a few tendrils hanging to caress her cheeks. She walked to Anthony.

"You are the most beautiful girl in the world." He stated.

He handed her a box. Inside was a white carnation wrist corsage. He took it out of the box, slipping it onto her wrist.

"No flower could do justice to your beauty." He declared and gently kissed her cheek. Tears welled in her eyes. Another rustle was heard at the top of the stairs. All heads turned to look at Abby. She wore a peach gown that left her shoulders partially bare. Beneath were slippers of gold that gently contrasted with her gown. She carried a delicate gold handbag.

The gown shaped her body to perfection. It was nipped in at the bodice to show off her figure and mold her firm, supple breasts. The skirt flowed over a petticoat. Her hair had been plaited and coiled atop her head like a coronet. A few tendrils had been left to dance along her face.

Kyle stepped forward, draping an arm over the banister, planting one foot on the bottom step naughtily. Abby floated down the stairs to his outstretched hand. When at last she came to the bottom, he took her hand. Courtly he raised it to his mouth as he held her eyes with his.

"Permit me my lady, to offer this sorrowful token of my affections." He drawled, showing her a pale peach rose.

He pinned it to the bodice of her gown, brushing one sensitive nipple with the back of his hand. She took in a small breath. No one wanted to break the spell Kyle wove around himself and Abby. In the softest tone anyone ever remembered hearing him use, Samuel said, "Your grandmother asked me to give these to you."

He held a box out to each Abby and Andrea. Inside each box lay a string of white pearls. Taking hers off its bed of satin, Abby offered it to her grandfather. "I'd be honored if you'd help me with these Granddaddy." She said through tears.

Samuel made a courtly bow to Abby and Andrea before he placed a necklace against each of their bosoms.

"After tonight I'll have to lock the two of you in a tower." Andrew stated.

All laughed, then left for the ball. Entering town hall, they were announced.

"Master Samuel Phillips."

"Master and Mistress Andrew Phillips."

"Master Anthony Caldoni escorting Mistress Andrea Phillips."

"Master Kyle Masterson escorting Mistress Tabitha Phillips."

Everyone gasped at the sight Abby and Andrea made. For a moment the room was silent, then everyone began to whisper. Abby spotted Eric and Jessie. Without thinking, she let out a small giggle.

"What's so funny?" Kyle asked as they walked across the room.

"Uh, nothing." Abby said through another giggle. "I'll tell you later." Eric and Jessie walked toward them.

"I see you didn't take my advice about your gown, Abby." Jessie said jealously.

"I'm happy to see you took mine. Scarlet really is your color." Abby said politely.

Jessie turned red. Kyle laughed, but turned it into a cough. "Perhaps we should get something to drink." He suggested.

"That's a good idea." Eric agreed.

Abby let Kyle lead her to the refreshments.

"Was it my imagination or did you just call Jessie a scarlet woman?" He asked as they walked to the refreshment table.

"It wasn't your imagination, you heard correctly. When Andie and I came to town to shop for the ball Jessie and I sort of had words." Abby told him.

"That's why you giggled when we came in." Kyle stated. Abby nodded. The next few hours were spent socializing and dancing. Kyle talked to the residents of Shelby, getting their reaction to having K. M. Enterprises come to town. He danced with Abby and other women. He warned Richard away from Abby. The Spring Ball Queen, Junior Division was chosen. Abby crowned her. Following, Mayor Collins announced the candidates for Spring Ball Queen, Senior Division. Each entrant was asked a question and escorted around the hall. They stood at the front of the hall once again.

"After careful consideration, we have selected a new queen. Drum roll, please." Mayor Collins said.

He took the envelope from his wife. "And our new Spring Ball Queen, Senior Division is..."

He opened the envelope. "Mistress Tabitha Phillips." Everyone applauded.

"I have the honor of crowning this year's queen." Mayor Collins said, after the applause died down.

Abby walked to where he stood. He placed a diamond tiara on her head.

"Mistress Phillips will now take her coronation walk."

Kyle stepped forward, offering his arm. As they walked around the room to applause Kyle leaned in to whisper, "They did choose the most beautiful woman."

Abby smiled up at him, squeezing his arm. After finishing the walk, they were asked to dance in the spotlight. Kyle swept Abby into his arms. Abby took off her tiara putting it back on its bed of velvet and sat it on the front seat of Kyle's Candy Apple Red Corvette. Jessie threw her venomous looks all evening.

"Would you like to go for a drive?" Kyle asked helping Abby into his car when the ball was over.

"That would be wonderful. Yes, thank you." Abby told him, looking lovingly into his eyes.

Kyle saw the look but chose not to comment. If only I can get her to admit she loves me. He thought. They drove through town. He stopped at the edge of town at Lover's Hill.

"How did you know about Lover's Hill?" Abby asked.

"I overheard some teenagers talking about it and asked directions." Kyle answered.

Abby believed him. Only Kyle could do something that ridiculous and not sound foolish. He pulled her toward him, "I've wanted to kiss you all evening." He growled softly.

"What's stopping you?" She asked.

"Not a damn thing." He pulled her closer to capture her lips. Demanding everything he put his hands on her waist to pull her onto his lap. Together they reached the height of passion. The car became uncomfortable, they went out to the grass. Kyle had a double sleeping bag in the trunk in case of severe weather. He took it out and spread it on the cold ground. He easily undressed Abby, swiftly discarding his own clothing. Inside her, he left no part of her untouched by his lovemaking. He molded her to him. His hands roamed from her soft, firm breasts to her pliant, supple bottom. He began very slowly bringing

Abby to the edge then back again. Finally she could take no more, "Now, Kyle, please love me now." She whimpered.

"Only too happy to love you, my lady." He said.

He took her over the edge to a place she'd never been. Afterwards he lay with her in his arms. She promptly fell asleep, snuggled to the hard contours of his body. He pulled the sleeping bag around them.

"God, send her back to me. I love her more than life itself." Kyle said just before he too fell asleep.

He deliberately hadn't taken any precautions against Abby getting pregnant. Later he awoke to see the sunrise before him. "Abby, wake up." Kyle shook her gently.

Abby opened one eye, then the other and slowly sat up. "Isn't it beautiful?" She said when she saw the beauty of the sunrise. She shivered in the cold morning air.

"Not as beautiful as you." He said as he caressed her bare shoulders.

"We should get back to the house." She said hesitantly. "I know, let's stop for breakfast first." He said.

"All right."

Kyle helped Abby dress.

"How do you wear these things?" He asked.

"Women will go through almost any torture to be beautiful." She teased.

"You don't have to torture yourself for me."

"Oh, you!" She said, slapping at him. "Help me here, then we can have breakfast and go home."

They stopped to have a leisurely breakfast and went home.

"About time you two came home." Andrew grumbled when they walked in.

"We didn't mean to worry you Daddy. We went for a drive after the ball then stayed to watch the sunrise and then had breakfast." Abby explained.

No one mentioned the dark spots on their clothing where it had lain in the snow.

"You're home now that's all that matters, isn't it Andrew?" Judy said. Andrew mumbled under his breath.

"I think I'll go take a nap." Abby said sleepily, smothering a yawn.

# CHAPTER FOUR

Kyle and Eric returned to Atlanta the following week, Kyle to meet with the team responsible for opening the Shelby Division of K. M. Enterprises and Eric to start tying up loose ends so he could move back to Shelby.

Abby thought about Kyle more than she was willing to admit. She stayed busy to avoid thinking about him making love to her. At work it was easy she had things to keep her mind occupied. When she wasn't working there was nothing to distract her.

Kyle had been in Atlanta for a few weeks when he called. "Abby?" He asked when the receiver was picked up.

"No, Kyle, this is Andrea. Hold on I'll get Abby." Andrea said. Putting her hand over the receiver she said, "Abby, phone. It's Kyle." Abby's nerveless fingers dropped the spade she'd been using. Wiping her hands on her jeans she went into the house.

Picking up the phone she said, "Hello, this is Abby."

"Hi, Querida. I need you to find a building for me. You have two weeks. I'll be there as soon as I can to look at it." He gave her the square footage the building needed to be and hung up.

"That man." Abby said slamming down the phone.

"What's wrong?" Andrea asked, looking up from the book she was reading.

"He wants me to find a building for him." Abby said. "What's the problem?" Andrea asked.

"Andie, Kyle couldn't find the building he needs when he looked, what makes him think I can?"

"Kyle hasn't lived here all of his life, you have. He obviously trusts your judgment."

"I'm not one of his flunkies to be commanded, he could have at least asked."

At work the next day, Abby asked her boss if he knew of anyone who had building space to lease. He told her of the few he knew of. She looked at them on her lunch break.

The next few weeks were busy for Abby. She spent her time working and trying to find a building for Kyle. She dreamt about him at night.

Two weeks passed, Abby hadn't been able to find a building for Kyle. She was tired after working all day and looking at buildings after work. Kyle called to check on her progress.

"How are you progressing on the building?" He asked.

"I've looked all over but nothing is right. I'm going to look again this afternoon." Abby told him.

"I'm sure you'll find something. I have confidence in you. I should be there in a few days, Love." The line was disconnected.

She picked up the stapler from her desk intending to throw it. Thinking better of it, Abby returned it to its place on her desk. When she left work Abby drove around again to look for buildings. She discovered a building set back from the road. Pulling into the drive, she wondered how she had missed it on her previous excursions through the area. Stepping out of the car, she walked to the front of the building.

Turning the knob on the door she found it locked. She walked around the building to look through the windows. They were dirty and grimy from years of neglect.

She went back to her car and drove to the realty office where one of her high school classmates worked. Going inside she spoke with her. Describing the building and its location, she asked who owned it.

She was told she would have to speak to one of the agents before they could tell her who owned it. They might not be handling the sale.

Abby arranged a meeting with an agent for the following afternoon. She met the agent at the appointed time and was told the agency was handling the sale. Going to the building, the agent took her inside. When Abby asked what the square footage was, the agent said they'd have to go back to the office to find the listing. It was perfect for Kyle, at least to begin with. When Abby arrived home she looked up K. M. Enterprises in her address book. Finding it, she called Kyle. A young woman answered, "K. M. Enterprises, Atlanta, May I help you?" She said.

"Kyle Masterson, please." Abby responded. "Whom may I say is calling?" The woman said. "Tabitha Phillips." Abby told her.

Kyle was on the phone immediately. "Yes, Tabitha, may I help you?" He asked in a business like tone.

"I've found a building for you." She told him. "Have you?" He said.

"Yes, Kyle what's wrong with you? I thought you'd be pleased." She said.

"Of course I am. We're having a meeting about it right now. I'll call you when it's over." He hung up.

Abby picked up a pillow from the couch and threw it across the room. Andrea walked out of the kitchen and was hit in the stomach.

"I'm sorry, Andie. I didn't know you were there." Abby apologized. "Talking to Kyle again?" Andrea guessed.

"How did you know?" Abby asked puzzled.

"ESP? A problem?" Andrea said facetiously.

"You don't have ESP. It's nothing I can't handle. I'll be back later." Abby told her.

Abby walked in the grassy meadow. She'd done what she'd told Kyle she hadn't wanted to. She'd fallen in love with him.

"I have to get away, but where can I go?" She said to herself.

She thought and thought. When she went back to the house she wasn't any closer to having a solution to her problem. Kyle returned her call.

"Have you seen the inside of the building you've chosen for me?" He asked when Abby picked up the phone.

"Yes Kyle, if you didn't trust my judgment why did you ask me to do the job?" She snapped.

"I trust your judgment, Querida. Tell me about the building." He said. Abby described the building with enthusiasm and related the information the agent had given her. He asked endless questions. She gave answers.

"It's filthy from standing empty for so long, but it can be cleaned." "Is the foundation sound?"

"Yes, the agent said it's a very good building. The owners want to sell it as quickly as possible."

"I'll see you as soon as I can get things cleared up here." He hung up. A week later Abby was coming in the door when the phone rang. "Abby, is that you?" Judy asked.

"Yes, Mama." Abby answered. "There's a call for you."

"I'll get it in here."

Abby picked up the receiver. "Hello, this is Abby."

Expecting Kyle to answer on the other end, she was surprised to hear the female voice come over the line.

"Abby, it's Aunt Millie. How are you?" Millie said.

"I'm fine, Aunt Millie. How are you?" Abby answered.

"I have a bit of a problem. I need a Personal Assistant."

"What happened to Connie?"

"She ran off and eloped. Ungrateful child. After all I did for her." Abby laughed.

"How can I help?"

"I think it's fairly obvious. I want you to come to Atlanta."

"You want me to come to Atlanta? Aunt Millie I can't, I have a job here."

"Pooh. You can give your boss notice and come to Atlanta in a month."

Abby took time to think. She wanted to get away. This was her chance. She quickly calculated the time.

"I should be able to be there in three weeks."

"Fine, I'll see you in three weeks." The line was disconnected.

"Aunt Millie offered me a job this afternoon." Abby said at supper that evening.

Andrew and Judy pretended surprise. "What sort of job?" Andrew asked. "Personal Assistant." She told him.

Andrew really was surprised, "Personal Assistant? What happened to Connie?" He asked.

"She ran off and eloped. Ungrateful child. Aunt Millie's words not mine."

The following day Abby gave two weeks' notice to her boss.

"I don't know how I'm going to manage without you. This office would have been a mess without you." He told her.

"I'm sure your new assistant will manage things as well as I have, if not better. I'll stay long enough to train her." Abby assured him.

Abby began to pack for her move. She only packed those things that were essential, stacking her boxes in a corner of the living room. Kyle came back amidst her packing.

"What's going on?" He demanded when he saw the boxes in the corner.

"I'm moving." Abby told him.

'Where are you moving to?" He asked.

"Out of state. I've been offered a job. I'll be leaving in a little over two weeks." She informed him.

She was in the center of the boxes. He couldn't reach her unless he went through the maze. He'd just found her after nearly five years he couldn't lose her again.

"You can't leave. What kind of job have you been offered? I'll pay you double the offer, but you'll have to stay in Shelby." Kyle commanded.

"I can and will leave. I will not stay here and allow you to finish what you started in Atlanta." She told him.

Abby saw the look of pure rage in his eyes. She was grateful for the boxes that surrounded her. She was aware however, if he had a mind to, he'd just toss the boxes out of his way.

"I'm going to the Pub." He said and slammed out the door.

Abby shook uncontrollably. Tears filled her eyes. She let them fall. Kyle wanted her, but he didn't love her. She'd go to Atlanta, make a new life for herself and forget him. Atlanta was a big city, how hard could it be to avoid him? She went to her room, crying herself to sleep. When she awoke she climbed out of bed and went to take a shower, putting her robe on afterward. She decided to get something to eat before she finished packing. Her parents were in the kitchen when she entered.

"Good afternoon." She said.

"What went on here this afternoon?" Andrew asked harshly.

"What do you mean, Daddy?" Abby stalled.

"I mean Tabi, Kyle came into the Pub mad as a hornet. He was mumbling something about having an argument with you. When I left he was drinking enough for two men." Andrew informed her.

"Goodness, I didn't realize it was a crime to have a disagreement." Abby said.

"What disagreement?"

"He told me I couldn't take the job with Aunt Millie. I told him he couldn't order me around."

The next few weeks went by quickly while Abby prepared to move. She spent her time working, packing and helped Kyle close the deal on his building. Abby and Kyle had many disagreements about her move. He forbade her to leave. She told him he couldn't run her life. She gave her family specific instructions not to tell Kyle where she was going.

Finally the day for her to leave arrived. She refused to let anyone take her to the airport; she didn't want a tearful good-bye. She promised to call when she arrived at Millie's. Millie met her at the airport.

"How was your flight?" Millie asked.

"It was fine, Aunt Millie. Did my things arrive?" Abby asked.

"They arrived a few days ago. Now, tell me about the young man you're running away from." Millie said.

"I'm not running away from anyone. You sound like Kyle. What makes you think it's a man?" Abby said to her.

"Your Mama told me about the young man, Tabitha. She said you met him when you came here after your disastrous affair with Richard."

"I would hardly call my relationship with Richard an affair."

"But you're not denying the affair with this young man. I can see it in your face."

Abby started to protest, but Millie continued, "An affair is nothing to be ashamed of, as long as your lover isn't married. Let's get you settled in, then you can tell me all about him."

They were settled in the library of Millie's home, Abby having called her parents, having tea.

"All right Tabitha, I want to hear all about the young man who has stolen your heart." Millie demanded."

"Aunt Millie no one has stolen my heart." Abby protested.

"I want to make something perfectly clear, young lady. I am not feeble-minded, nor am I blind. You never were a very good liar. If you want my help, you're going to have to be honest with me. Now about this young man."

"Kyle."

"And his surname?"

"Masterson."

"Kyle Masterson, such a romantic name. Is he a good lover?"

"He's a wonderful lover, but Aunt Millie..." Too late Abby realized her mistake.

"You tricked me." She accused.

"Of course I did, Dear. Admitting to being lovers is the first step to admitting how you feel. Now about Kyle."

"Oh, what's the point? I came to Atlanta to get away from him."

"You came to Atlanta to get away from him? Doesn't he live here?"

"Yes, he bought a house shortly after I met him. Atlanta is a big city."

"Getting back to my point. You're in love with Kyle."

Abby opened her mouth to interrupt, Millie sent her a quelling look and she closed it again.

"Remember, I told you if you want my help you're going to have to be honest."

Abby nodded, and then said, "Aunt Millie I am in love with him. But it's pointless I don't want to be in love with him."

"Pointless? By that do you mean he isn't in love with you?"

"I know he wants me, like some sort of trophy. I honestly doubt he loves me."

"He wants a trophy?' Millie said thoughtfully. "If it's a trophy he wants that's what we'll give him."

"Aunt Millie I will not be any man's trophy. That's why Richard wanted to marry me, remember."

"Of course not, Dear. We only have to make him think you are a trophy, so he'll come after you."

"Make him think I am a trophy? That doesn't make any sense; besides, I don't want him to come after me. He doesn't know where I am."

"No need to quarrel with me Tabitha. It'll be easy enough to let him know where you are. As for not wanting him to come after you...of course you do, if only to attempt making love to you again."

Abby stared at her aunt with wide eyes. Several times she opened her mouth to speak, only to close it again when nothing came out.

Several minutes passed. Deciding her niece had had enough time to reject anything she'd said, Millie poured more tea into their cups.

"First we have to attract him to the prize. We'll start with your appearance."

Abby looked at herself. Finding nothing wrong with the way she looked, she protested. "What's wrong with the way I look?"

"Nothing, if you're a colorless old maid. The colors are all wrong and the style doesn't flatter you."

Millie began getting information about Kyle. Abby gave answers. She was amazed at the way in which her aunt got the information she sought. If Abby didn't answer directly, Millie simply rephrased the question so she would get the answer she was seeking. Abby hadn't been aware she knew so much about Kyle. She realized she must have paid more attention than she had first thought to Eric when he spoke about Kyle on his visits home.

As afternoon became evening, Abby became more confused than she had in any other time in her life. They ate supper while Millie ferreted out information on Kyle. Later when Abby climbed into bed she went over the afternoon's events trying to understand what had happened. Understanding no better, she drifted into a sensual dream about Kyle. Morning came too soon for her. She struggled to stay inside her dream. Millie shook a little harder when she realized Abby was struggling between her dream and reality.

"Wake up, Tabitha. We have a lot to do today." Millie said.

Slowly opening her eyes, Abby tried to focus on her aunt's voice. "Aunt Millie?" She asked in a gravelly voice.

"Of course, child, who did you expect?" Millie asked. Abby smiled lazily and slid deeper into the comforter.

Millie smiled. She pulled the covers off the dozing young woman and tipped the mattress on its side. Falling to the floor, Abby instantly came awake.

"All right, Aunt Millie I'm awake."

"About time too. We're already an hour behind schedule." She became lost in her own thoughts.

"Aunt Millie, are you listening to me?"

"I'm sorry, I was lost in thought. What did you say?" "I asked why you pushed me out of bed."

"We have things to do and I want to get started. Breakfast in twenty minutes."

Twenty minutes later Abby had showered, dried most of the water from her hair and was dressed. She went downstairs to greet her aunt a proper good morning.

"By the smile on your face this morning, I trust you slept well." Millie stated.

"Yes, I slept well. How was your night?" Abby said, smiling. Millie smiled. "I slept like a baby."

Abby was taking a drink of her orange juice and nearly choked on it. "You have a lover!"

She hadn't meant to speak her thoughts. Nor did she know how she knew, on the other hand, maybe she did.

"I am discreet about it, but you are correct." Millie told her. "I don't think we should talk about this."

"I'm helping you now because I had no one to help me when I was young and in love."

"Your personal life is none of my business, Aunt Millie."

"If telling you about my past will help you, I will."

"I, uh, I'm not sure that's such a good idea. I mmmean...Aunt Millie you're doing it to me again."

"I'm not doing anything to you. I'm going to teach you how to share your feelings. You've bottled them up for nearly five years, it's time to let go."

Millie let the thought sink into her niece's head before she continued.

"Neither of us has reason to be ashamed that we have a lover. The only shame would be for you to lose yours because you can't forget the past."

"Hadn't we better get started?"

Leaving a short time later Millie took Abby to the best shops in Atlanta. They stopped at Millie's hair salon to have Abby's hair trimmed and to get beauty tips for her. All morning and afternoon Abby tried to slow Millie down.

"Aunt Millie you can't do this." Abby said.

Millie said, "It's what I want to do. Hush up and do as you're told." When they went home that evening they were happily exhausted.

"I'm going to have to find a place of my own." Abby said over supper.

"Whatever for? Don't you like staying here?" Millie asked.

"I love staying here, but you can't want someone under foot after living by yourself all these years. Connie didn't live with you."

"Connie isn't my niece. Besides, we couldn't live together; we're too much alike. I'm glad to have someone to talk to."

After supper Abby and Millie took their day's purchases to Abby's room. After putting them away, Millie bid Abby good night. Abby spent the rest of the week settling in at Millie's. It was agreed she would stay there for the time being. The next week she began her job. After a few days of working for Millie, she decided she liked being a Personal Assistant better than she had a Legal Assistant. All was going well for her and she loved working for Millie. One morning she woke up nauseous. She ran to the bathroom. Going down the stairs, she smelled breakfast. It was enough to send her running back up the stairs. Ten minutes later she went to greet her aunt.

"Good morning, did you sleep well?" Millie asked.

"I slept like a baby, but I woke up nauseous." Abby told her.

"Nauseous? Do you feel sick? Are you coming down with something? Should you take the day off to rest?" Millie inquired.

"I'm sure it will pass." Abby said.

The nausea didn't pass, in fact it became worse. Over the next few weeks she noticed her clothes were too tight.

"How are you feeling, Tabitha?" Millie asked one evening.

"Not very well.  The nausea hasn't passed and now my clothes are too tight." Abby told her.

Millie looked Abby over. Guessing at the reason for her niece's discomfort, she asked, "How are you feeling otherwise?"

"Now that you mention it, I have noticed an increase in my appetite. Why do you ask?"

"Oh, no special reason. I'll call Dr. Cooper in the morning to set up an appointment."

Abby agreed to see the doctor.

# CHAPTER FIVE

Abby went to the doctor appointment Millie set up for her.

Dr. Cooper asked general health questions and asked a nurse draw her blood.

"When was your last monthly cycle?" He asked. "I don't remember, let me check." She answered.

Abby pulled her calendar from her purse. Looking at the dates, she turned white and told Dr. Cooper the dates.

"Have you always been on time? Is there any reason you would be late?" Dr. Cooper asked.

"They've always been regular. I've been under a lot of stress lately." Abby told him.

"I'll call you at your aunt's with the results of your blood test." He said.

'Thank you." She said.

Abby walked to her car in shock. Driving home she was aware of very little.

The phrase 'I'm expecting Kyle's baby' kept running through her mind. When she walked into the house, Millie asked, "How was your appointment with Dr. Cooper?"

"You knew, didn't you? That's why you sent me to see him." Abby accused.

"Knew what?" Millie asked curiously. "That I might be pregnant!" Abby cried. "I didn't know exactly. I suspected."

"Why didn't you say something? You could have at least warned me."

"It wasn't my place to tell you. Didn't you suspect?"

"Of course not. If I had suspected I would have seen the doctor before now. I put uh...things down to stress. How am I going to explain this to Mama and Daddy?"

"I'm sure you won't have to explain it to them."

"You know what I mean, Aunt Millie. How could this happen?" "I'm sure your mother had that little talk with you."

"Aunt Millie! I know how it happened. I don't understand how it could have happened. I thought Kyle would have taken precautions, especially after..."

"They are not guaranteed, Tabitha."

"I know that!"

"Didn't you take precautions?"

"Me? How could I have known this would happen?" Abby said, walking out of the room.

"Where are you going?"

"To get something to eat, I'm starving."

Abby went to the kitchen followed by Millie's laughter. When she finished eating she went to her aunt's study to work. When the phone rang she tensed and ignored it. Millie appeared in the doorway.

"Dr. Cooper's office is on the phone." She said.

"I'll take it in here." Abby told her.

Millie nodded as Abby reached for the phone. "Hello, this is Abby Phillips." She said.

"This is Dr. Cooper's office. We have the results of your tests." The nurse said.

"Yes?"

"Congratulations you are about two months pregnant."

"Thank you."

"Would you like to make an appointment to see the doctor?" "I'll call back in a few days." Abby hung up.

She had known she was pregnant, but she was still shocked at the confirmation. Millie came into the study.

"What did the doctor's office say?" She asked.

"You know perfectly well what they said." Abby snapped.

"Ignoring her niece's anger, Millie said, "When is the baby due?"

"I think around Christmas time."

"A Christmas baby, how wonderful."

"What would you say if I decided not to have the baby?" Abby asked. "Not have the baby? You mean you're considering abortion?"

"I didn't say that."

"Then why ask such a foolish question? Of course you'll have the baby."

"How am I supposed to raise a baby on my own? I can't stay here forever. I certainly can't go home and I won't go to Kyle."

"No one said you had to stay here forever. I'm sure my brother would welcome his grandchild, but I would never force you to go home. As for Kyle, he is the baby's father. Doesn't he have the right to know about his child?"

"I don't know if Kyle likes children, let alone wanting any of his own." "Relax for a few days, it'll all work out. Now that we've learned that you're pregnant we'll have to change our plans."

"Forget your plans, Aunt Millie. Promise me you won't do anything until I've decided what I'm going to do."

"You know me better than that."

"Yes, that's why I want your promise." "Now, Tabitha..."

"Don't now Tabitha me, I want your promise, Aunt Millie." Millie opened her mouth to protest. Abby glared at her.

"Oh, very well. I promise I won't do anything until you've decided what you're going to do."

"Thank you."

Abby called her parents to let them know how she was doing. Deciding no time would be better than the present, she told them about the baby.

"You're going to have a baby? You'll come home right away." Andrew decided.

"No, Daddy, I'm not coming home. Kyle is there. He'll be traveling back and forth between Shelby and Atlanta at least until the end of the year. I don't want him to know about the baby yet. I haven't decided if I'm going to tell him." Abby said.

Andrew smiled. "What do you mean you haven't decided if you're going to tell him? Doesn't he owe it to you and the child to take responsibility for his part in your condition?"

"He isn't there is he?"

"No, he left a little while ago to do some work at the office."

"Don't tell him. He may do something I'll regret."

"What would he do?" Judy asked.

"Offer to marry me." Abby answered.

"Would that be wrong? He is the baby's father." Judy reminded her.

"I don't want him to marry me because I'm pregnant. He doesn't love me." Abby told her.

"Did you know you were going to have Kyle's baby when you left? Is that why you wanted to leave?" Andrew demanded.

"No, Daddy. I left to get away from Kyle."

"Have you decided what you're going to do about the baby?" Judy asked.

"I'm going to have the baby, Mama. Please don't tell anyone outside the family."

Judy and Andrew let out the breath they'd been holding.

"We'll keep the baby a secret for now, but remember you can't hide your condition indefinitely." Judy told her.

"I'm not trying to hide it, Mama. I need time to think things through." Abby hung up.

She called Dr. Cooper's office to set up an appointment for pre-natal care. Having done that, she felt better. After seeing how tired Abby was after working all day, Millie moved supper back an hour. This enabled Abby to take a nap when she completed her work for the day. The days blended into weeks. Abby went shopping for maternity clothes. She thought about Kyle every day. Her body began to show changes little by little. Her breasts became tender, her abdomen began to swell, and she looked radiant. Abby talked to Millie about the baby. She told her how much she wished to tell Kyle about her love and the baby. She cried herself to sleep at night for the love she carried in her heart and womb.

It became a daily habit for Millie to ask Abby how she was feeling. She did so one evening after they'd finished work for the day. Abby burst into tears going to her room. Millie followed.

"What's wrong, child?" Millie asked.

"I don't know, Aunt Millie. This is supposed to be one of the happiest times of my life. Why do I feel so miserable?" Abby asked.

"Tabitha, it's raging hormones. The feelings are normal. Everything will work out. You rest, after supper we'll take a walk."

After Abby rested, they ate supper and went on their walk. They walked in the park near Millie's house. When Abby grew weary they sat on a nearby bench. They were talking when Abby suddenly had a prickling sensation on the back of her neck. She looked up to see Kyle walking toward them. He hadn't seen them yet. She turned white. Noticing her pallor, Millie became concerned.

"Tabitha, you're pale what's wrong?" Millie asked.

"K-Kyle, he's coming this way!" Abby stammered.

Millie turned around to look in the direction Abby was staring.

"He can't know about the baby, Aunt Millie. What am I going to do?" Abby pleaded.

"Leave everything to me. Pretend we're having an engaging conversation." Millie told her.

Millie turned to face Abby and sat so she was blocking her almost completely from view.

Kyle walked by them, almost missing Abby. "Querida, is that you?" He asked surprised.

Abby looked up. Pretending surprise, she said, "Kyle, how are you?"

"Fine, what are you doing in Atlanta?" He asked. "I'm working for Aunt Millie I live here."

She made the introductions.

"It's nice to meet you, Kyle. I've heard so much about you." Millie told him.

He arched a brow at Abby.

"My nephew Eric talks about you quite often. He admires you very much." She said, drawing his too curious gaze away from Abby.

Kyle was looking oddly at Abby. Her face was fuller than he remembered it. It could be due to the change in her appearance since she'd come to Atlanta. Or was she pregnant? Millie was preventing him from getting a complete view of her.

"Are you all right, Querida? You look a little pale." He said.

Abby looked at him sharply. "I'm fine. I'm just a little tired. I haven't been sleeping very well." She answered.

She had to get away from him before he started asking more questions. How could she get away without letting him see her protruding stomach? Looking at her watch, Abby said, "It's getting late, Aunt Millie. We should be getting home."

She pulled her cloak down, so she could at least try to keep Kyle from getting a glimpse of her swollen abdomen as Millie stood and brought her fully into his view.

"You have an open invitation for supper anytime, Kyle. My address is in the book." Millie said as she stood.

"I'll call before I stop over. May I stop by tomorrow evening?" Kyle said.

"That would be lovely. We'll make a special supper for your visit." Millie said as Abby dragged her off.

"I'll look forward to it." Kyle said after them.

"Seven o'clock." Millie told him.

"I'll be there."

"How could you do that Aunt Millie? I don't want him popping in whenever the urge strikes him. I can't hide my pregnancy from him indefinitely!"

"You worry too much." Millie replied.

The next evening by six thirty Abby had tried on every one of her maternity dresses at least twice. She couldn't find one that didn't have a neon sign flashing and pointing out her condition.

"Aunt Millie, I'm going to have supper in my room tonight." She said as her aunt dressed in her own room.

"Shall I send Kyle to eat with you?" Millie questioned mischievously.

"Of course not; I'm trying to hide my pregnancy from him, not draw attention to it." Abby told her.

"Then I suggest you get dressed before he arrives. He's coming to supper to be with you, not me." Millie told her going downstairs.

Abby had the urge to stamp her foot like a child. She gave into the urge, twice. Grabbing one of the dresses laying across her bed, she pulled it on. With a little bit of adjusting and a lot of cursing, she looked at herself in the mirror. It would have to do. Kyle rang the doorbell promptly at seven. Taking a deep, calming breath Abby answered it.

"Good evening, Kyle. Won't you come in?" She said sweetly.

"Good evening, Querida. You look enchanting this evening." Kyle said as he bent his head to kiss her.

Abby allowed him to briefly kiss her. He gave her the flowers he had brought her. Taking them, she said, "Thank you, they're beautiful," inhaling their scent. She showed him into the living room.

"Can I get you a drink?" Abby asked.

"Scotch." He answered.

Abby filled a glass with ice and poured the Scotch into it.

She walked to Kyle, handing the glass to him. His fingers brushed hers when he took the glass. She wasn't surprised, expecting his touch whenever he was near.

"I'll put these in some water." She said, indicating the flowers. She went to put them in water. Kyle sat on the couch.

"How are things going?" Millie asked when Abby walked into the kitchen.

"Peachy, I'm never going to make it through the evening." Abby told her.

"Of course you are." Millie said.

Abby gave her aunt a skeptical look while she put water in a vase she'd found in the cupboard. She put the flowers in the vase and took more time than was necessary arranging them.

"It isn't polite to keep a guest waiting." Millie reminded her.

"I'm going, I'm going!"

Abby walked back into the living room. She sat the flowers on an end table.

"How is the new factory coming along?" She asked.

"Very well, we have most of the staff hired. You already know the renovations are nearly complete." He answered.

She nodded. "Eric told me, congratulations. When will the factory open?"

"As soon as we finish hiring the staff and Eric can wrap up his affairs here. Probably by the end of October."

"That soon, Eric said it wouldn't be until the end of the year."

"We expected it to be the end of the year, giving us enough time to find the building we needed."

"You found it before you expected to?"

"Actually you found the building. We didn't expect you to find one so soon. We were able to speed things up when we closed the deal on the building."

"You told me you needed that building in two weeks."

"Yes."

"Why?"

"To offer you a job in our legal department. As Office Manager you'd be expected to handle the mundane jobs. I offered you a challenge and you passed."

"Of all the conniving, backhanded...I didn't ask for a job."

"Tabitha, a lady never raises her voice." Millie said walking into the room.

"To hell with being a lady. I'm going to check on supper." Abby stalked out of the room.

"I just checked on supper." Millie told her.

"I may need to add something...maybe some arsenic." Abby said. Kyle's laughter followed her all the way to the kitchen.

"This is very good." Kyle complimented as they ate. "The arsenic adds just the right flavor."

Abby had the grace to blush.

"Abby made supper. I'm not much of a cook. Before she came to live with me I mostly ate take out or friends took pity on me." Millie told him. Their meal started with a salad containing banana and apple slices. The dressing was made from sugar and Miracle Whip. The main course was a roast Abby had cooked in cream of mushroom soup, which they used as gravy. Green beans also cooked in cream of mushroom soup and mashed potatoes completed the meal. For dessert she had made strawberry cheesecake from scratch.

They were having coffee in the living room. Thus far Abby had been successful in hiding her condition from Kyle, but the strain of her secret was getting to her. She was having a difficult time keeping up with the conversation. After her third attempt at trying to grasp the conversation Kyle and Millie were having, she sat back and gave up. Her dress pulled against her abdomen showing evidence of her pregnancy.

Kyle didn't miss the swelling of her stomach before she hastily rearranged her dress to cover their child. Seeing Kyle's gaze drift to her, Abby's hand automatically came up to protect their unborn child.

"Abby are you pregnant?" Kyle asked angrily.

She drank her coffee too quickly and started to choke. In one quick movement Kyle was at her side.

"I think I'll leave you two alone." Millie said, rising to leave the room. Abby looked beseechingly at her. Millie pretended not to see.

"I asked you a question, Querida." Kyle reminded her, after Millie had left the room.

"As you already know the answer, there's no sense in my answering you is there?" Abby said.

"Why didn't you tell me?" He demanded.

"I wasn't sure how you'd react. As it is, you're angry." She defended.

"I'm angry because you didn't tell me. I'm going to be a father, yet you didn't tell me. Why?"

"I knew you'd offer to marry me. I didn't want an offer of marriage out of your misguided sense of obligation."

"What about my right to know that our affair created a child?" "I didn't want you to think I'd trapped you."

"You didn't trap me." He said too quietly. "What?" She said alarmed.

"I said you didn't trap me. I didn't take any precautions against you conceiving our child."

"You purposely tried to get me pregnant?"

"Yes."

Abby stared at him, not believing what she was hearing. It was there in his eyes, he was telling the truth. He had found the one way to tie her to him that could never be broken.

"Get out! Get out before I..."

"Before you what, Querida? There's nothing you could do to me that I haven't already done to myself."

Abby went up the stairs to her room. Kyle started to follow, but Millie stopped him.

"Leave her to sort things out." She told him.

"What have I done? She'll never forgive me. I never meant to tell her this way." He said dejectedly.

"She loves you. She'll forgive you. Give her time."

"She loves me. Abby won't consciously tell me, not of her own free will."

"What happened the night you met Tabitha?"

"I don't know. All I do know is that she ran away from me. It took me nearly five years to find her, I can't lose her again."

"Give her time." Millie repeated.

"I don't have time. Every day that passes brings me closer to losing her forever. I thought a baby..."

"I'll have her home at the beginning of November. You have until then to come up with something."

"That will be enough time."

Abby was resting after supper three weeks later when she felt a little jab in her abdomen. She sat up.

"Is anything wrong?" Millie asked.

"I'm not sure. I think I felt something." Abby told her. They waited. Nothing happened.

"I must be imagining things. Does it say anything in those books you've been reading about losing your mind during pregnancy?" Abby joked.

"I don't think you're imagining things. The books say you'll feel something, then you won't feel it again for several days." Millie reminded her.

The next few days Abby kept expecting to feel the baby move again.

When it didn't she became depressed. Abby and Millie had by tacit agreement not mentioned the supper Kyle had been to, or the events that had followed. During one of her doctor's visits the doctor looked for the baby's heartbeat. He thought he detected more than one. He asked her to have an ultra sound done. When the results came back, he looked apprehensively at Abby.

"Is something wrong?" She asked.

"Nothing unusual. I believe you're expecting twins." Dr. Cooper told her.

"Twins, I'm going to have twins?" Abby asked dumbfounded.

"It'll be a few months before we'll know for sure, but I'm ninety-five percent positive you're expecting twins." He said.

Abby didn't remember the drive home.

"How did your appointment go today?" Millie asked when Abby came in.

"I don't know how to tell you this." She was silent for a long time. "Is something wrong with the baby?" Millie asked concerned.

"Oh, no, Dr. Cooper thinks I'm expecting twins. It'll be a few months before he can be positive." Abby told her.

"Twins? That's wonderful news." Millie said.

"Kyle will be getting more than he bargained for when he took the risk of getting me pregnant." Abby said unconsciously.

Startled, Millie looked at her niece. She saw that Abby wasn't aware she had spoken aloud. She let the remark pass without comment.

Abby felt the babies move frequently.

Late summer turned into early fall. The leaves were falling off the trees. September ran into October. Abby hadn't seen Kyle since they'd had supper with him and he'd dropped his bombshell. She guessed he was busy with K. M. Enterprises, Shelby Division. Millie felt no need to tell her that Kyle called regularly to get reports on her health and condition. It would only have upset her. She decided to take Abby out for her birthday.

"What would you like to do for your birthday?" She asked.

"Nothing special." Abby said.

This would be the first time she would celebrate without Andrea. She had talked to her and their parents that morning.

"There must be something you want to do." Millie insisted. "I'd like to forget my birthday." Abby said irritably.

The doorbell rang. Millie went to answer it.

"Tabitha, it's for you."

Abby walked to the door. On the front lawn stood a group of young men from a local fraternity. When she appeared in the doorway, they sang Happy Birthday. Followed by Slow Hand, a Conway Twitty song. The first song Abby and Kyle had danced to on the night they met. A young man was also standing to the side of the door.

"This is for you miss." He said handing her a long box with a card attached. Abby absently took the box. He tipped his hat to her and joined the others on the lawn. She opened the box. Inside lay a half-carat opal surrounded by diamonds on a delicate silver chain. She lifted the card from the box. It said:

Sending birthday wishes your way for all of your dreams to come true. Happy Birthday, my Love

All my love, Kyle

"Oh my." Abby gasped.

Millie waved the young men away. She turned to Abby and helped her put on the necklace.

"Now, what would you like to do for your birthday?" Millie asked again.

"Whatever you decide will be fine." Abby told her, rubbing the opal between her fingers.

They went out on the town that night and slept late the next morning. Abby had begun her seventh month of pregnancy. She was getting excited. Her mood swings were typical of a woman in her condition. October blended into November. It was getting colder.

"How would you like to go home?" Millie asked.

"Aunt Millie I'm not going anywhere. I'd just scare people, I look like a blimp." Abby said.

"Tabitha Rae Phillips, are you so selfish that you'd deny your parents a visit from you?" Millie argued.

"Aunt Millie you know I can't go home, Kyle may be there." Abby reminded her.

"He's probably in Atlanta. He did tell you the Shelby Division would be operating at the end of October. I'm going to the travel agency tomorrow. You've been stuck in this house too long. You need your mother now."

Abby was on a plane flying home. She was excited. She dozed on the plane she tired easily lately. Dr. Cooper told her it was a normal part of pregnancy. Millie didn't tell her Kyle was still in Shelby. When the plane landed Millie shook Abby awake. Groggy, she sat up. They departed the plane. Millie spotted Kyle and Eric before Abby. She directed her toward the luggage carousel when Kyle saw them. Kyle started forward. Eric held him back.

"She isn't likely to welcome your presence." Eric told him. "Why?" Kyle asked.

"She doesn't know you're here." "Why not?"

"Aunt Millie wouldn't have gotten her on the plane if she would have told her you were still here."

"She'll just have to get used to having me around. She's expecting my child. I'm going to take care of her whether she likes it or not."

"Kyle, don't do anything you'll regret. Abby could run off and there would be nothing you could do to stop her."

"I'll just have to make sure she doesn't run off, won't I?" Eric opened his mouth to speak.

Kyle warned him that Abby and Millie were within hearing distance. "Good afternoon, gentlemen." Millie said.

Abby turned toward them. Her knees buckled. Kyle was there to catch her.

"I'll take her to the car." He said.

"You'll do no such thing. You'll put me down, I'm getting on the next plane back to Atlanta." Abby hissed. Turning to her aunt, "You lied to me. You told me he was in Atlanta."

"I didn't lie to you, Tabitha. I neglected to tell you he hadn't left Shelby." Millie told her. "Your mother invited him to join us for Thanksgiving Dinner."

"As much as I enjoy being the topic of conversation, I think you should postpone this particular conversation. Abby needs to get off her feet." Kyle said sarcastically.

They went to the car and started on their way.

"I'll just turn around and go back to the airport." Abby warned Kyle.

"I'm not letting you out of my sight until we've decided what to do about the baby." He said.

"Babies." Abby corrected.

"Babies." Kyle repeated dumbfounded.

"Yes, we're expecting twins. I'm surprised my big mouth brother didn't tell you that too. He has told you everything else about me."

"Your family hasn't told me anything, exactly as you instructed. "Everything I've learned about you, I've found out on my own."

"You're not going to play guard dog while I'm home. I won't be kept a prisoner."

"I'm going to make damn sure you don't run off with my children before they're born. I have rights, I'm going to exercise a few of them while I can."

"You can't keep me here if I don't want to stay."

"Watch me. If I have to tie you in bed until my children are born, I will."

He kissed her.

"Abby you look radiant." Judy told her when they walked through the door.

Abby blushed.      She didn't know if her radiance came from Kyle's kisses or impending motherhood.

"Thank you, Mama." She said.

"How are my grandchildren?" Andrew asked.

"You're grandchildren are fine, Daddy. Dr. Cooper gave me a clean bill of health before we flew home." Abby told him.

"You shouldn't be on your feet. Sit down, get comfortable." Andrew told her.

"Comfortable isn't part of my vocabulary. I'll settle for mild discomfort." She said.

Everyone laughed; the evening was spent talking. When it was time to go to bed, Kyle took Abby's elbow as he helped her up the stairs. They bid everyone good night. Kyle walked past her room.

"What are you doing?" She asked.

"I asked your mother to put you in my room. I told you I wasn't letting you out of my sight until we decided what to do about the babies."

"Of all the arrogant, manipulative, sneaky..."

"I get the  picture, Querida. You're not happy with the sleeping arrangements I've made. Nevertheless, they won't be changed."

They came to his door. He extended his hand, indicating that she should enter first. Holding her head high, she walked into the room. Her suitcases sat on a trunk at the end of the bed. Opening one, she pulled out an oversize cotton nightgown. Going into the bathroom, she slammed the door. Kyle followed.

"What are you doing?" She asked.

"I would think it's fairly obvious. I'm getting ready for bed." He answered.

"You can damn well wait until I'm through!" She snapped.

"I'm not leaving you alone until I have a guarantee you won't run off."

"It's not likely I'm going anywhere. We are on the second floor and I am eight months pregnant."

"Arguing isn't going to get us anywhere and I'd like to get some sleep. "You'll have to tolerate my presence; it'll be permanent soon." He told her.

Abby stepped into the shower, closed the doors and disrobed, throwing her clothes over the top. Stepping away from the showerhead, she turned on the water. She adjusted the temperature and stepped under the water. Strong hands massaged her tense shoulders. She gave a start. Abby hadn't heard Kyle step into the shower, and her senses telling her that he was near seemed to have deserted her. He ran his hands down the length of her. Pulling her to him, he massaged the place where his children lay. Taking the bath gel and pouf in his hands, he ran the soapy pouf over her. He washed and conditioned her hair. When he finished, she tried to return his attentions.

"No, Querida, I can't endure your touch."

Refusing to let him see how his rejection had hurt her, she said, "I'm going to get dressed. Suddenly I'm cold."

"I'll be out in ten minutes." He said.

Abby stepped out of the shower. Taking a towel out of the linen closet, she dried and pulled her nightgown over her head. Kyle turned off the hot water. He had to get his body under control. Being near Abby had brought him to full arousal. He'd had to get her out of the shower before he made love to her. He wouldn't take the chance of hurting her or his children.

Going back into the bedroom, Abby took out her brush and carelessly ran it through her hair. Walking to the bed, she pulled back the covers and climbed in. Lying on her side, she forced back the tears. She wouldn't cry. She just wouldn't. Kyle couldn't endure her touch. She knew why. Her pregnancy made her unattractive to him. Why had he insisted she share a room with him?

"To be certain I don't run off with his children." She answered.

She sat up, swinging her legs over the side of the bed. Getting up, she started walking toward the door. The bathroom door opened. "Where are you going, Querida?"

"To my own room." She told him, hating the tremor in her voice.

"Why?" He asked when he saw that she'd been lying in his bed.

"You find me unattractive. My pregnancy offends you." She whispered.

He was beside her quickly. "Where did you come up with that idiotic notion?" He demanded.

"I am not an idiot Kyle Masterson! You can't endure my touch. You said so yourself." She threw at him.

He pulled the towel from his waist and threw it across the room.

"Look at me, Sweetheart. See for yourself what your nearness does to me." He commanded.

Involuntarily, her eyes strayed to his arousal. "Oh."

"I won't take the chance I might hurt our children..."

She looked away from him. He took her chin in his hand and forced her to look at him. "Or you." She saw tenderness in his eyes. He hugged her to him.

"Come to bed, love. At least I can hold you in my arms while we sleep." He said softly.

When they got into bed he held her close. Abby was restless.

"What's wrong, Darlin'?"

"I can't get comfortable."

She sat up pulled a pillow from behind her, put it between her knees and laid back. Cradling her in his arms, he felt her relax and finally she slept. She was home, in his arms.

In the morning Abby awoke to an empty bed. Kyle had arisen early; the pillow was cold where his head had rested. Sitting up, she was about to climb out of bed when the door opened. Kyle came in carrying a tray laden with food.

"Good morning, Darlin'. How did you sleep?" He greeted.

"Good morning, Kyle. I slept like a rock." She said, scooting to sit up against the pillows.

He set the tray across her legs. "I made this with my own two hands, so you better eat it. You wouldn't want to hurt my feelings." He told her cockily.

She wanted to wipe the smirk off his face. "Is it edible?" She asked humorously.

His smile slipped until she laughed.

He stepped toward her menacingly. "Yes, it's edible you little minx." He growled.

"Now Kyle, you wouldn't want to waste all this food."

Kyle and Abby shared the breakfast of pancakes, ham, eggs, juice, coffee and toast he had prepared.

Afterwards they dressed and joined everyone downstairs.

# CHAPTER SIX

Kyle was unexpectedly called back to Atlanta for a crisis. Abby drove him to the airport.

"I'll be back as soon as I can, Love. Take care until I get back?" Kyle said.

"Yes Kyle, I'll see you when you get back." Abby promised.

He took her in his arms to give her a kiss that would stay with her until he came back to her, then he walked to his private plane and boarded. Abby watched the plane until it was out of sight. She turned around to go back to her car.

"Hello, Abby." Richard said.

"What are you doing here?" Abby asked surprised.

"I've been having you followed." He informed her.

"Having me followed? Why?" She asked.

"I want to talk to you. Now that your lover is gone, I have my chance. That scene I just witnessed was very touching. I do hope you gave him a proper good-bye." He told her.

He took her elbow to lead her out to his car.

"What do you want to talk about?" Abby asked.

"Our marriage." He said.

She began to panic. He was crazy. She knew better than to struggle with him, he could become violent.

"Our marriage?" She asked.

"Yes, you've had your little fling. Now it's time to settle down and get married...to me."

"But I'm expecting another man's children."

Richard was momentarily surprised. He hadn't been told she was expecting more than one baby. He quickly recovered.

"Merely a small problem to be dealt with. We'll tell our children you became pregnant during an affair after running away from our wedding."

This wasn't the Richard she knew. He would never accept another man's children as his own. What is he up to? Abby thought to herself. They were in his car driving down the highway. She couldn't jump out of the moving car, even if she weren't eight months pregnant. He'd just turn around and come after her.

"Where are you taking me?" Abby asked.

"Don't bother your pretty little head with the details. You have enough to worry about." He told her.

"Damn it Richard, where are you taking me?"

His eyes left the road to look coldly at her.

"Ladies do not swear, Abby. I told you not to worry your pretty little head."

He returned his attention to the road. She had to keep him talking until she thought of a way to escape.

"I don't have anything to get married in."

"I've taken care of everything."

"Damn!" She had to find a way to let her family know Richard had kidnapped her. They wouldn't be expecting her back for a couple of hours. An idea came to her.

"Richard, can we stop to get something to drink?"

He looked at her suspiciously. "This had better not be a trick to get out of your promise to marry me."

"I'm thirsty. My doctor told me to drink several glasses of juice and water every day."

It was only half a lie. He didn't know she wasn't really thirsty. When they came to a rest stop, Richard pulled in. He walked up to the building with her, handed her change for the vending machines and said,

"Get me a Coke. I'll be right back," then walked off towards the men's room.

Abby watched him walk in. Now was her chance. She walked to the vending machines, dropped in some coins, pushed one of the buttons and retrieved Richard's Coke. She walked over to the pay phone, dropping in some change. She punched in her parents' number while watching the men's room door. She hastily explained to her mother that Richard had kidnapped her. Judy listened without interruption. Richard came out of the men's room and became angry when he saw Abby on the phone.

Abby smiled, holding up his Coke.

"That's right, Mama. Richard and I are finally getting married." Abby told Judy.

Judy took the hint that Richard was nearby. Abby listened while her mother spoke. Richard took the Coke from Abby, grabbing for the phone. Abby turned away so it was out of his reach. With her free hand she linked her fingers with his, repressing the tremors at the contact.

"No, I don't know when we'll be getting married. Richard wants to surprise me." Abby said.

Abby smiled at Richard.

The anger left his eyes. He lifted her hand to his mouth, kissing the back.

Abby fought down the shudder that threatened to run through her body. She listened to her mother speak again.

"Yes, we'll call again as soon as we can, Mama."

Abby hung up the phone. Turning back to Richard with a false smile, "I hope you aren't angry with me. I had to call Mama to tell her that we're finally getting married."

"I thought you might be calling for help. I know you wanted your family to be with you when you married. We'll get married again in church after you have the babies."

Abby nodded. He started walking back to the car. "My drink?"

"I'll get it. You go back to the car."

Abby walked back to the car and got in. She looked in the ignition. Richard had taken the keys. He came back to the car loaded down with drinks. She looked at him questioningly.

"So we don't have to stop again." He explained.

Abby had told her mother which direction Richard had driven when they'd left the airport. Now it was up to her family to find a way to thwart Richard's plans. She leaned her head against the seat. Sleep claimed her. Eric called K. M. Enterprises headquarters in Atlanta.

"K. M. Enterprises Atlanta, may I help you?"The receptionist answered.

"Get Kyle Masterson on the line now!" Eric commanded.

"Whom shall I say is calling?" She asked.

"Never mind. This is an emergency! Get him now!" Eric barked.

"Yes, sir." was the reply.

There was a pause, a click and Kyle was on the line. "This better be important." Kyle barked.

"Kyle, Richard has kidnapped Abby." Eric told him.

"What? How?" Kyle demanded.

"When she was leaving the airport. He intends to force her to marry him." Eric said.

Eric gave Kyle the details.

"The son-of-a... I'll have my pilot turn around."

Kyle hung up. He called his brother Quinton to take care of the crisis in Atlanta, explaining he had a personal emergency to attend to. He ordered his pilot to fly back to the airport near Shelby immediately.

"Dear God, keep her safe." He whispered.

Richard shook Abby awake. "We're here, Darling." "Here? Where?" Abby asked sleepily.

"My cabin. We'll stay here for a few days and discuss our plans for the future, then we can get married."

Abby stumbled from the car. She held onto the door as a wave of dizziness overtook her.

"Are you all right?" Richard asked.

"Yes, fine. I think I stood up too fast." She told him. He led her into the cabin.

"Sit down, I'll bring the luggage in and fix you some tea."

Abby nodded, walking to the sofa to sit down. He went to the car to get the luggage.

"I hope you like the trousseau I've chosen for you. The saleswoman said you'd love it." He told her, while taking their suitcases out of the trunk. Carrying them into the cabin, he said, "This is your room."

He walked into the room he'd indicated. She followed him into the room wanting to take a shower.

"I'd like to take a shower." Abby told him.

He nodded, showing her where the linens were.

"After your shower you can drink your tea and unpack."

"Unpack? Yes, of course, my trousseau."

"See how well I take care of you? I even do your shopping. We're going to have a wonderful life together."

Richard went into the kitchen to make tea. Abby prepared to take a shower. He didn't act as though he intended to harm her. But he was insane if he thought she was going to marry him. She'd have to sit and wait for her family to find them. The babies picked that moment to become restless. Kyle! She hadn't thought about him since leaving the airport. Would her mother tell him that Richard had kidnapped her? Would he rescue her to save his children?

After her shower, wrapped in a towel, Abby opened one of the suitcases to find a robe. It was peach, with a tie at the waist, and light blue piping on the sleeves and hem. She put it on and wrapped her hair turban style in a towel. Richard appeared in the doorway.

"Feeling better?" He asked.

"Yes, after my tea I'll feel even better. I'm a little nervous." She admitted.

"Bridal jitters. I promise we'll be married soon. You unpack while I make supper."

"Okay."

*"How am I going to stall him until Kyle can find us?"*

Richard told her his plans for the future. She was his prisoner and could do nothing but wait. He told her to eat, she ate. He told her to sleep, she slept.

Abby's nerves were at the breaking point. She became physically ill as the stress of the situation got to be too much for her. Richard put her to bed, sitting next to her almost constantly. He left only to bring more cool cloths to bathe her face, and hot tea or broth for her to drink.

"I'm sorry, my Darling. If I'd have known waiting to be married would cause this, we'd have been married right away." He told her, encouraging her to drink the broth he was holding.

Hoping to make her feel better, Richard put his engagement ring on her left hand. It fit snug because of the weight she'd gained during her pregnancy. Abby was too weak to protest. When she was able to sit up for short periods, without waves of dizziness, Abby tried to talk to him.

"I have to see a doctor, Richard. The babies have to be checked."

"I'll take care of you and the babies. Rest for a few days. We'll make our plans when you're feeling better."

He left the room to make her more tea. Abby slapped her hand down on the bed in frustration. During the next few weeks Abby became more of a prisoner. Richard watched for signs of improvement in her condition. When he brought up the subject of marriage, she used her weakened state to ward him off.

"But you are better. You said so yourself." He whined.

"You don't want me to have a relapse do you? This is my first pregnancy and without a doctor...who knows what might happen. You wouldn't want me fainting at the altar." She pointed out reasonably.

Abby thought she was dreaming Kyle came to rescue her. He was holding her hand, whispering that he loved her.

"Querida, wake up. Please wake up. I love you." Kyle said. The nurse came into the room.

"I'm afraid you'll have to leave sir." She said.

"I'm not leaving her until she wakes up." He said.

"The rules..."

"I don't give a damn about your rules. I'm not leaving her side until she orders me out."

Abby had been brought into the hospital only hours ago. Kyle refused to leave her side. He and Eric had talked to Richard's parents explaining the situation to them. They had agreed to help in any way they could.

Gene Dalton had been the one to tell them about the cabin. It had taken he and Eric nearly a week to find the place. When they had finally located the cabin, Kyle had wanted to storm in. Eric had talked him out of it. "My wife and children are in there." Kyle said.

"Abby isn't your wife yet Kyle. I'm going to call the police." Eric told him.

"In my heart Abby has been my wife since the night we met. No police. There's no way of knowing what he'll do. I don't want him alerted to our presence." Kyle ordered.

Eric had had to agree with Kyle to stop him from rushing in. Watching the cabin, they immediately noticed something was wrong. They hadn't seen Abby, only Richard.

"Do you suppose he's tied her up?" Eric asked.

"No, he knows she wouldn't get far in her condition. Abby wouldn't take the chance something would happen to our children." Kyle said. When they finally went in to rescue Abby she was asleep and unharmed. Richard put up very little resistance. Nevertheless, Kyle got in one good punch that sent him across the room. Eric pulled him back before he could do any real damage. Kyle found Abby in one of the bedrooms. She woke up when he walked into the room.

"Kyle?" Abby said groggy.

"Yes, Querida it's me." He answered.

He cradled her in his arms, telling her that their children were safe. He took Richard's ring off her finger, putting it in his pocket. Abby fell asleep again and hadn't awakened. Eric took Richard to the police.

Kyle took Abby to the nearest hospital. The doctor in the emergency room had assured Kyle that Abby would be fine.

"She's had a terrible shock, her body is helping her get the rest she needs. When she's rested, she'll wake up." He said as a matter of fact. The doctor checked the babies; they were going to be fine.

Kyle heard the nurse talking to someone in the hall. "Has he been in there all this time?" Andrew asked.

"Yes sir. Says he won't leave until she wakes up and orders him out." The nurse said.

Andrew walked into Abby's room and saw Kyle holding her hand.

"You look like hell, boy. Go back to the hotel and clean up. I'll call you when she wakes up." He said.

Kyle stared at Andrew with haunted eyes.

"I'm not leaving until she wakes up. She doesn't have the strength to fight. I've got to be strong for her." Kyle told him.

"You're not going to do her any good exhausting yourself. I'll call you when she wakes up."

"Nothing could make me leave her. Dalton got to her the last time."

"Richard is in jail. It's not likely he'll be getting out any time soon. He's been convinced it's the safest place for him."

The voices Abby heard came from a tunnel. She struggled to break through the foggy mist that surrounded her wooly brain. She let the fog claim her. Her mind must be playing tricks on her. She'd heard Kyle, but he was in Atlanta.

Kyle left her room once in the two days she'd been there. The nurses finally convinced him to get some rest. He agreed to let Judy relieve him the day after

Abby had been brought in. When he came back into the room, Abby was sleeping fitfully, tossing and turning.

"What's wrong?" He asked.

"She knows that you weren't here." Judy told him.

"Now that she hears you, she's sleeping peacefully." The nurse said.

Kyle looked at Abby. She was resting peacefully.

"I'm not leaving her again."

That was yesterday. Kyle couldn't believe it had been such a short time ago. Judy came into Abby's room.

"How is she today?" She asked.

"The doctor says she's doing better." Kyle said.

"She should wake up soon. Why don't you go get something to eat? I'll come get you when she wakes up."

Kyle started to protest. Abby stirred once again, fighting the foggy mist that threatened to engulf her. She refused to let it claim her this time. Kyle noticed the change in the way she was holding his hand. She squeezed his hand as if to gather strength from him. She tried to speak, but her throat was tight and dry. She licked dry lips. Kyle leaned in to hear her. "Darlin'?"

Abby gave him a frail smile when she recognized his voice. "Don't tire yourself. Do you want something?" He asked.

"Water." She said, barely a whisper.

He leaned in to hear her.

"I'll get the nurse to bring her some water." Judy said. Kyle nodded.

Judy left to get the nurse.

"How are you feeling?" Kyle asked.

Abby tried to answer her throat was coated with sandpaper.

"Never mind. You rest the nurse is bringing water."

She squeezed his hand again. The nurse brought Abby water. She drank greedily. The nurse only allowed her a few sips.

"Slowly, Mrs. Masterson." She said. Kyle and Judy looked at her in surprise.

"I told my supervisor you're her husband. If I hadn't she wouldn't have let you stay." She explained.

"Thank you." He said to her. She nodded and left.

Abby opened her eyes. The light hurt, she closed them again.

"I'll call the family to let them know Abby is awake." Judy said. Kyle nodded. He held Abby's hand she fell asleep again.

Abby was in the hospital a few more days. When she awoke Kyle was there to give her water, hold her hand and talk to her until she slept again. Her family came and went. Kyle left for short periods to eat, take showers and change clothes. She slept peacefully when he was near and fitfully when he wasn't. Thanksgiving Day was three days away.

Abby was sitting up in bed when Kyle came back into her room. He leaned over, brushing her cheek with his lips.

"How are you feeling today, Querida?"

"Stronger."

"The doctor says if you behave yourself you can go home in a few days."

"Really?"

"Uh huh."

Abby was released the day before Thanksgiving. Kyle picked her up and assured the doctor he'd make sure she didn't overdo. Abby tried to help make Thanksgiving Dinner. She was continuously shooed out of the kitchen and told to rest. "Would anyone like to play Trivial Pursuit?" Abby asked.

The Chicago Bears were playing the Detroit Lions at the Pontiac Silverdome at Pontiac, Michigan. They were playing the traditional Thanksgiving Day football game. All of the men, with the exception of Kyle, were watching the game. He offered to be her opponent. She accepted. Abby and Kyle had been playing the board game for a while when the babies moved. She moved in her chair to find a comfortable position.

"Abby are you all right?" Kyle asked.

"Considering my condition, I'm fine. The babies are moving. I'm trying to adjust their position." She told him.

His eyes lit up.

She saw his interest and asked, "Would you like to feel them move?" Kyle held back the joy he was feeling at her question.

"Are you sure?" He asked.

"Come over here."

She placed his hands on her swollen stomach.

"Wait a few minutes and you should feel them move."

They were quiet, holding their breath. The babies kicked, knocking a surprised Kyle on his backside.

"My sons have quite a kick." He said.

"Do you want sons, Kyle?" Abby asked.

"Every man wants a son to carry on his name, but I'd be just as happy with daughters. Were you going to keep them from me, Abby?"

Abby started to get out of her chair. He was in front of her almost as soon as the thought occurred. Abby was getting annoyed at the way Kyle kept reading her mind.

"No Abby, I won't let you run away again. I want answers." She thought over his question.

"I didn't know I was pregnant when I went to work for Aunt Millie. I was just as surprised as you when I learned I was carrying your child."

Kyle sat back in his chair. "Why didn't you tell me you were pregnant when the doctor told you? Or the night we met in the park?"

"I didn't know what I was going to do. I hadn't decided whether or not to tell you."

He stared at her for so long she thought he hadn't heard her.

"You've made all of the decisions concerning our children, I'm going to make one. I'm giving you two weeks to prepare for our wedding."

"You're no better than Richard, with his plans to force me to marry him. Besides, I won't marry a man who doesn't love me."

Telling her now that he loved her would be futile. She wouldn't believe him if he told her in front of a judge and jury, and they pronounced him guilty.

"Love has nothing to do with it. I'm exercising my rights."

"You can't force me to marry you. You're conveniently forgetting the rights you took away from me when you decided to make me a baby factory."

His eyes were colorless points of anger. He reached over, grabbing her by the arms.

"I didn't decide anything. An opportunity presented itself, I took advantage of it."

"You took advantage of me."

He let his hands drop. "No. We were talking about my rights. Either you marry me or we have a custody fight. Your choice."

"If I decide to marry you, it will be in name only."

"I'd rethink my decision if I were you. Going to court could be a long and expensive battle. You marry me and sleep in my bed. I will not tolerate a marriage in name only."

"That's blackmail."

"No, it's strategy. One year is all I'm asking. After that...we'll cross that bridge when we come to it."


"One year! I don't want to be married to you for five minutes, let alone one year."

Judy announced dinner. Everyone headed into the dining room.

"Let us bow our heads in thanks to God for his many blessings." Andrew said when everyone gathered at the table.

After the prayer, Andrew stood. "Now we'll share what we're thankful for." He announced.

Samuel started, and then it went to Judy and Eric. Millie went next, then Andrea. Andrew shared what he was thankful for. Kyle and Abby remained. He invited her to go first. She declined.

"I'm thankful Abby has agreed to marry me." Kyle said boldly. Surprise was audible around the table.

"I haven't yet agreed to marry you, Kyle." Abby said defiantly.

"Well, why not?" Andrea insisted on knowing.

"Excuse me." Abby said.

She stood and left the room, followed by Kyle, going to the room they shared.

"Are you happy now? You've just made it impossible for me to explain why I don't want to marry you." She accused.

"That was the reason for doing what I did. When I want something, I don't stop until I get it." He pointed out.

He put his arms around her, holding her close. Kyle smelled and felt good. Abby could hear his heartbeat. She clung to him as she listened to what his heart was telling her. She didn't hear the natural cadence of a heart, but the words of one heart talking to another.

"All right Kyle, you win. I'll marry you."

Kyle held her for a while longer, sending a thankful prayer heavenward. He bent his head and kissed her, running his hands the length of her body. She was softer and rounder than she had been.

"Shall we go back down to dinner?"

Abby nodded.

During dinner she was offered each dish at least twice. "No time to count calories." Samuel scolded.

"Drink your milk it's good for the babies." Andrea reminded her.

"Don't use so much salt, it isn't good for the babies." Judy reprimanded.

After dinner Kyle took Abby for a walk. He linked their fingers while he held her hand.

"What would you have done if I hadn't learned of your pregnancy, Querida?" Kyle asked.

She wasn't surprised at his question.

"I would have raised our children alone, if necessary." She answered.

"What do you mean by 'if necessary'?"

"I have the feeling we were brought together by an unnatural force."

"We were manipulated? No one manipulates me."

"Believe it or not Kyle, you couldn't have prevented it if you'd have tried. What would you have done if I'd told you about my pregnancy?"

"I'd have offered to marry you. What kind of man do you think I am?"

"Instead you blackmailed me."

"I used strategy to get what I wanted. Would you have married me willingly?"

"I don't know...I always thought I'd be in love with the man I married."

*Meaning you aren't in love with me*, Kyle thought.

"Look at marrying me as being out of love. Love for our children. Did you think I'd let you raise them on your own? I am responsible for them."

"In more ways than one." She mumbled.

"Did you say something?" He asked.

"Just talking to myself."

They walked in silence thinking their own thoughts.

Marrying Kyle was going to be the hardest thing she'd ever wanted to do. Strategy or force, Kyle's plans were nothing like Richard's. She wanted to marry Kyle because she loved him, but under better circumstances.

Their walk had taken them around the block. They stood in the front room of her parents' home.

"Are you going to tell your family about our marriage?" She asked.

"Tell my family?" He asked, searching her face.

"Are you going to tell them we're getting married?"

"Oh, not until we get to Atlanta. My mother is on a cruise. Quinton, my brother, is taking care of the crisis in Atlanta. My father is too busy to be bothered."

"You're going to spring it on them after the deed is done."

"You act as though it's a dirty secret I have to hide from the world."

"Have you told them you're going to be a father?"

"No, I haven't..."

"You haven't told them. Who's ashamed of our affair Kyle, you or me?"

Without waiting for his answer, Abby went up the stairs to their room. He started to go after her, running into Millie. Millie had come into the living room and witnessed the scene.

"What's wrong with Tabitha? You didn't have a lovers' quarrel did you?" She asked hesitantly when she saw Kyle's angry expression.

"Lovers' quarrel? We are about as far from being lovers as it is possible to get!" Kyle snapped.

"You have been lovers and you will be again." Millie said positively.

"She doesn't trust me and it's not likely she ever will." He said losing patience.

"She's marrying you isn't she?"

"I threatened her with a custody battle if she didn't agree to marry me." His pensive gaze followed Abby's trail up the stairs.

"You can't force my niece to do something she doesn't want to. She loves you."

"Why does she push me away when I get close?"

"She's been hurt by two people whom she thought loved her. Tabitha feels she needs to protect herself against loving you."

"Of all the nonsense... she's mine I'll not so subtly remind her." He slammed out the door.

"Kyle needs to learn to keep his temper under control." Andrew stated.

Millie spun around, not surprised to see her brother standing in the doorway.

"How long have you been standing there?" She asked.

"Not long enough, but long enough to know he's too sure Tabi will surrender to his possessiveness." Andrew remarked.

"What do you think we should do?"

"We can't do anything more. We've gotten her to Atlanta, Kyle has convinced her to marry him. The rest is up to them."

# CHAPTER SEVEN

Abby paced the room she shared with Kyle. The two plus weeks since Thanksgiving had been busy. Kyle booked the church and asked the minister to marry them. Ironically, he was the same minister who would have married her to Richard five and a half years earlier. Judy secured town hall for the reception. Andrea dragged Abby to the shopping mall, finding the perfect dress for Abby to wear for her wedding. Ginger Dalton had insisted that Abby take the trousseau Richard had bought for her. Telling her it was the least they could to make-up for the trouble he'd put her through. Abby hadn't lifted a finger in preparation of her wedding, yet she felt she had been rung through a ringer.

"It's time to go to the church, Abby." Andrea said, poking her head in the door.

"I'm not going. I've changed my mind." Abby told her.

"Very funny, you can no more change your mind about marrying Kyle than you can having those babies." Andrea stated.

Andrew proudly walked Abby down the aisle.

"Dearly beloved we are gathered here in the sight of God and these witnesses to join this man and this woman together in holy matrimony..." Abby heard the minister say.

After that she couldn't remember much else. The ceremony was short and in fifteen minutes they were pronounced husband and wife.

"Remember the last time we were here?" Kyle asked, twirling Abby around the dance floor.

"Don't remind me. We're here tonight because I decided to go to that damn ball." Abby told him.

"Say it a little louder I don't think the people in the corner heard you." He said harshly.

"I don't particularly care who hears me." She said.

"No one will suspect we aren't in love, especially not my mother."

"We mustn't let her think you married me to give your ba..."

"Don't say it, Querida. Never refer to my children by that name."

"Babies, Kyle, I was going to say 'to give your babies a name'."

Abby walked off the dance floor. Judy saw Abby walk away from Kyle and followed her.

"Is anything wrong, Abby?" Judy asked.

"No Mama, I'm just tired, I've had a long day." Abby answered.

"You've just married the man you love; this should be the happiest day of your life. Take some deep breaths then go make-up with your husband." Judy counseled.

Abby used the relaxation breathing she'd been taught in the Lamaze classes she'd taken.

"All right, I'm ready." She said.

They rejoined the party. Abby searched the crowd for her husband. Finding him, she walked over to him, linking her arm with his. Bending, Kyle gently kissed her.

"Are you all right?" He asked, lifting his head to look into her eyes. She hid her emotions from his too observant gaze.

"Yes, just tired from all the activity I guess." She answered.

"Let me know when you're ready to leave. My pilot is waiting at the airport." He told her.

Abby nodded.

Somehow in two weeks, Kyle had managed to give her the dream wedding she'd always wanted. His private plane was taking them home. Home. It had always been her parents' house or Aunt Millie's two-story brick house. Now she would share a house with Kyle and their children when they arrived. Abby laid her head on Kyle's shoulder. He put his arm around her, pulling her close. She was excited as well as apprehensive. Would he expect her to honor her promise to sleep in his bed? He'd made no demands on her before or after Richard had abducted her, only held her comfortingly while she slept. She had to get her thoughts off of making love with Kyle.

"How did you manage such a beautiful wedding in so short a time?" Abby asked.

"With hard work and initiative anything can be accomplished." He responded.

He had succeeded in making her wedding day special. He thought to himself.

Abby sighed tiredly.

"Rest for the remainder of the flight. We'll be home soon. We can talk later." He said.

Abby nodded and snuggled closer to him. When the plane landed Kyle helped her off. His driver waited for them inside the terminal. "How was your flight, Kyle?" Joshua asked.

"Fine, thanks Josh. This is my wife Tabitha." Kyle said.

"A pleasure to meet you, Mrs. Masterson." Josh welcomed her.

"I'm sure the pleasure is mine, Joshua. Everyone calls me Abby." She said.

"I like Tabitha, and I'm Josh." He told her.

He led the way to the waiting car after they'd collected their luggage. Josh pulled up in front of a two-story, ranch style house. When Kyle and Abby stepped into the foyer she smelled roses. The foyer and living room were furnished in coral and ivory.

"It's lovely, Kyle." Abby exclaimed.

Kyle looked around at the wonderful job the decorator had managed in two weeks. He'd had help from Judy and Andrea in choosing the soft, subtle shades Abby loved.

"I'm happy you like our home. If there's anything you'd like to change, feel free." He told her.

"What would I change? It's perfect." She announced.

"Would you like to see the rest of the house?" He asked.

"Can't we stay here, it's so peaceful."

Kyle laughed. "I guarantee you'll like the rest of the house." They toured the lower floor.

"How did you do it?" Abby asked.

He arched a brow at her question. "How did I do what?" He questioned, stunned that she'd guessed he'd had the house redecorated for her.

"Capture the sunshine and persuade it to stay."

"It must have followed you. Shall we go upstairs?"

"I'd like that."

He held her tightly as they climbed the stairs. They toured the upper floor. The color scheme was the same as it had been on the lower floor. He took her to the nursery first. She checked to see that it was fully stocked. It was.

"Would you like to see our room?" Kyle asked.

She hid her hesitation at sharing a room with Kyle in his home. Our home, she corrected automatically.

"That would be nice." She said absently.

They walked along the hall. Kyle opened the door to the master bedroom. Abby took a step back, coming into contact with the solid wall of his chest. She gave a cry of delight, turned around and threw her arms around his neck, nearly knocking him down. A king size, oak, four-poster bed with canopy dominated the room. A chest of drawers stood on one wall, a walk-in closet was on another and a fireplace was in one corner at an angle. French doors stood next to the fireplace, opening onto a balcony overlooking a natural spring. Behind the spring was a small forest of trees.

"Something wrong, Sweetheart?" He asked.

"Wrong? No, this is the picture that comes to mind whenever I think about my perfect bedroom." Abby said in a rush, tears forming in her eyes.

"You like it?"

"Like it, I absolutely love it. It's one of the most beautiful rooms I've ever seen. In fact the whole house is beautiful. Your decorator did a wonderful job."

"The house was redecorated recently. It was specially designed for..." Kyle cut himself off before saying "you."

"All except this room. My mother decorated in here when I bought the house five and a half years ago."

"She has excellent taste. Specially designed for who, Kyle?"

"It doesn't matter. I'm sure you'd like to unpack and get to bed. You've had a long day."

"Your day has been just as long."

"Yes, but I'm not eight and a half months pregnant. Which reminds me, who is your doctor?"

"Dr. Cooper."

"He's our family physician. I'll call his office Monday."

"Yes, of course you'll want to talk to the doctor about the babies' care. I'd like to rest now, I'm more tired than I realized."

"I'll bring up the luggage."

Kyle went down to get their luggage. Abby climbed into bed. Exhausted, but too keyed up to relax, she fell into a fitful sleep. Who had the house been specially designed for? He wanted to talk to Dr. Cooper about the babies. He wasn't interested in her; the babies were his main concern. After all, that was why he'd married her, wasn't it? Abby wasn't aware Kyle sat to watch her sleep when he brought up the luggage.

"Would he ever have her love or would she stay the required year and leave him again? No!"

The years fell away as he let the memories of the night they'd met invade his thoughts. Abby sat at a table in the corner. He'd walked over and asked her to dance. Leading her to the dance floor, Kyle had felt the first stirrings of desire as he looked into her chocolate brown eyes. They were a woman's eyes, just as her body was a woman's. They danced for a few hours as if they were the only two people in the world. Their bodies spoke the words unutterable to them. Holding her close was like heaven and hell for him. Kyle wanted her to himself, so made the excuse he wanted to leave the club. He took her hand in his, not wanting to break the contact they'd so carefully enjoyed. When they found themselves in front of his hotel, he'd selfishly led her into the elevator. He pulled her to him and kissed her. In the corridor leading to his room, Kyle pursued his desire.

Unlocking the door to his room, he'd pulled her into his arms and hadn't let go. Making love to her, he'd discovered she was a virgin and mentally kicked himself for rushing her. Abby had made light of the fact that he had been her first lover. When he'd found her missing from his bed the next morning, he'd abused the night clerk at the front desk until he threatened to call security.

Bringing his thoughts back to the present, Kyle went down to the study and poured himself a healthy dose of Scotch. When Abby awoke she was more tired than she had been when she lay down. Going downstairs she listened for signs of life. She heard nothing, but saw light filtering out from the study into the hallway. She walked to the doorway.

"Kyle?" She asked.

Slowly he looked in her direction. "Mrs. Masterson, good evening. You slept well I trust." He enunciated clearly.

"You're drunk!" She accused.

"No ma'am, but I'm trying my damndest." He announced holding up his glass in mock salute.

"I'm going back to bed. I suggest you sleep this, whatever it is, off." She told him.

"Don't mother me, Querida. Wouldn't you like to know why I'm getting drunk?"

At her look of derision, he continued, "I getting drunk because we were married today. Are we happily married, Darlin'?"

"I'm not going to discuss our marriage with you when you've been drinking. You won't find happiness in the bottom of a bottle." She told him and walked out. Halfway up the stairs she doubled over in pain. "Kyle, help." She cried reaching for the banister.

Kyle dropped the glass he was holding and ran to her side. The glass shattered, spilling its contents onto the floor.

"What is it?" He asked.

"I don't know. Sharp pain. Can't catch my breath." She said breathless.

He gathered her in his arms. Stepping around the broken glass, he carried her to the sofa in the study and laid her down.

"How are you feeling now?" He asked.

"Call the doctor, babies are coming." She panted.

Kyle went to the phone. He punched in Dr. Cooper's number.

"Dr. Cooper please, this is an emergency." He barked at the operator who answered.

"Yes, sir, right away." The operator said.

Several minutes went by. Kyle soothed Abby and mentally cursed the operator who had put him on hold.

"This is Dr. Cooper."

"Doc, this is Kyle Masterson. My wife is having twins. Her name is Tabitha. You'd know her as Tabitha Phillips."

"She's not due for a few more weeks yet, but you can bring her into the hospital and I'll examine her."

"Kyle, baby coming now. I want to push." Abby said between contractions.

"Abby says there's a baby coming and she wants to push." Kyle said.

"Kyyyyyle!"

"Doc, send an ambulance. I have to go to my wife." Kyle urged, giving him the address.

He dropped the phone in its cradle and ran to Abby.

"How are you feeling, Darlin?"

"Wonderful. Water broke." Abby took a breath to get through the next contraction.

"Can I get you anything?"

"Help baby out. Head coming out."

Kyle removed her wet clothing as quickly as he could. He began to panic as he saw the evidence that one of his children was about to be born. He realized he wouldn't be of any help to Abby if he panicked.

Forcing himself to relax, he said. "Tell me what to do, Abby."

"Can you see the baby's shoulders?"

"No."

"May need help. Cradle the head, gently pull help through."

Kyle did as he was instructed. After several minutes of pulling and cursing, he held his first-born.

"We have a son, Sweetheart." Kyle said holding his son close. He had his father's blonde hair and blue eyes.

"Wrap the baby in a blanket."

"In a minute. I want to hold our son."

She instructed him to suction out the baby's nose and mouth. Abby rested. Five minutes went by before the pains started again.

"We aren't through. Our other child wants to meet the world." This time Kyle talked Abby through the birth.

"We have a daughter, Baby." Kyle told Abby, tears of happiness evident in his voice.

She was identical to her brother. Kyle cleaned the baby's nose and mouth, and then wrapped her in a blanket. Afterwards, he settled his son and daughter in his wife's arms. Kyle wrapped Abby in the comforter from their bed. The ambulance came up the driveway, sirens blaring. It came to a stop in front of the house. Dr. Cooper came rushing in. What he saw amazed him. Abby lay on the sofa, wrapped in a comforter, while two small bundles lay sleeping in her arms. Kyle looked up as Dr. Cooper came in, followed by the Emergency Medical Team.

"You've done a fine job, Kyle." Dr. Cooper said. Abby opened her eyes and smiled.

Dr. Cooper set about his work. Soon mother, babies and an exhausted father were on their way to the hospital. Once there, Abby and the babies were taken up to the maternity ward. Kyle was handed over to the care of a nurse. She gave him strong, black coffee to counteract the Scotch he'd had to drink.

Later, a nurse awakened Abby.

"Mrs. Masterson, there's a young lady in the nursery who's quite insistent about being hungry." She said.

Abby smiled. "Please bring her to me."

The nurse went back to the nursery. Minutes later Abby was nursing her daughter. After nursing her, the nurse brought her son to her. She nursed him.

Finally, she was able to go back to sleep. Dr. Cooper left instructions that Abby have no visitors, except Kyle, and that she should rest as much as possible. The first few days she was in the hospital she slept. She had developed an infection; Dr. Cooper would release her when it was gone. Kyle remained by Abby's side, holding her hand. She squeezed his hand, when she asked for him he assured her he was there. On the third day, she was able to sit in a chair in her room. When she was climbing back into bed a nurse came in.

"How are you feeling today Mrs. Masterson?" She asked.

"Fine, thanks." Abby answered.

"Do you feel up to nursing?"

"Yes, please bring me my babies."

The nurse brought her babies to her. She put Abby's son in her arms. Abby cuddled him for a moment then nursed him. Kyle watched amazed, as his son instinctively knew what to do. Even though he'd seen it several times since his wife had been brought to the hospital.

"Amazing, isn't it?" He said.

Looking up from watching her son, Abby asked, "What?"

"How he knows what to do." He stated.

"Babies are amazing, Kyle." She told him, returning her attention to her son.

"That they are." He said leaning over to let his son grip his finger.

He brushed the rest of his hand against Abby's swollen, exposed breast.

Abby stopped the gasp that came to her lips at his sensual touch.

Kyle continued to caress her. She pretended to ignore him. Their daughter let her presence be known. Abby held their son out to Kyle.

He took him to put him back in his bassinet. He picked up their daughter, handing her to Abby. Before she could take her, Kyle cradled the baby in one arm. He bent his head to capture her exposed breast in his warm mouth.

Abby took a labored breath as he suckled. "Kyle, what are you doing?"

"I'm not sure. I couldn't resist. I'm sorry Querida, it won't happen again." He promised.

He gave the baby to her and walked out of the room. Abby nursed her daughter, all the while wishing Kyle would come back to finish what he'd started. They named their son Kerry Tyler and their daughter Kayla Rae.

A week later Abby was home settling into her children's routine. Kyle had hired Agnes to help with the house and babies. Abby went to find Agnes. Finding her in the kitchen, she sat at the counter.

"Kayla and Kerry are asleep." Abby told her.

"You look like you could use a rest yourself, Mrs. Masterson." Agnes told her.

"I'll rest after I have a cup of coffee. Where's Mr. Masterson?" Abby asked.

"He went out, he was acting mysteriously." Agnes informed her.

The Christmas holiday was approaching. It was a little over a week away. Abby hadn't finished her shopping. She used her breast pump to express milk for Kerry and Kayla.

Kyle's mysteriousness resulted in the most beautiful tree Abby had ever seen. It was a seven foot tall Douglas fir that sat in a corner of the living room next to the sleeper sofa. The tree was decorated with bows made of white ribbon, white crocheted fans, which Abby had made, three garlands of white Christmas pearls and four strings of all red lights.

Kyle insisted Abby take time for herself every day away from Kayla and Kerry. She was getting increasingly depressed as the holidays drew near. Dr. Cooper assured her it was normal after giving birth.

Kyle grew short tempered from the forced abstinence. Being near Abby, but not making love to her was physical torture. She withdrew from him at night when he tried to hold her. She'd seen lipstick and smelled perfume, not her own, on his clothes. He came home early one afternoon just as Abby was nursing Kerry. It was sweet torture to see part of her exposed breast.

"Must you nurse Kerry where everyone can witness?" Kyle barked.

She stared at him for a moment, then as regal as a queen she cradled her son to her and left the room. She went to the nursery to finish nursing her son. Afterwards, she checked on Kayla. Assuring herself that both of her children were resting, she went to her own room to lie down. When she awoke, she checked on Kayla and Kerry. They were asleep.

Abby went to start on supper. Agnes had started it. "What are we having for supper?" She asked.

"I thought we'd have something light. Homemade chicken soup and a salad." Agnes said.

"Sounds good. I'll see if Kyle is hungry." Abby told her.

"Mr. Masterson left about an hour ago." Agnes informed her.

"Did he say where he was going or when he'd be back?"

"No, just said to tell you not to wait up."

"I guess it's just you and me for supper."

"Yes, ma'am."

Abby and Agnes ate supper in silence. Abby wondered where Kyle had gone. Was he with a woman? The one whose lipstick and perfume she'd discovered on his clothes? Her heart refused to accept the thought; her mind couldn't deny the possibility. She fought the battle for several minutes. Her children's crying ended the battle she was having with herself. While Abby tended to her children she thought about Christmas. It would be the first Christmas she wouldn't be spending with her family. She couldn't go to Shelby; Dr. Cooper wouldn't allow her to travel yet. After nursing Kerry and Kayla she gave them their baths and put them to bed. Abby went to the phone and picked up the receiver several times to call her mother. Finally she punched in her parents' number. Andrea picked up on the first ring.

"Hi, Andie." Abby said cheerfully.

"Abby! How are you? How's Kyle? How are the twins? When are you coming home for a visit?" Andrea asked.

"Slow down, Andie. We're all fine. I don't know when I'm coming home. Dr. Cooper won't let me travel yet. That's why I'm calling, is Mama home?"

"Hold on, I'll get her."

"Hello, Abby, how are you?" Judy asked.

"Fine, Mama, how are things there?" Abby answered.

"This will be the first Christmas we won't all be together." Judy echoed Abby's earlier thoughts.

"I know."

"How are Kyle and my grandchildren?"

"They're all fine. Kayla and Kerry are asleep and Kyle has gone out." "I was hoping to talk to him. Have him call me when he gets home." "He may be home late, I'll have him call you in the morning."

"Does he go out often? Is he helping with the children? Are you getting enough rest?"

~ 151 ~

"Kyle is busy with work. He hired Agnes to help with the house and children and yes, I get plenty of rest."

"Kyle should be spending time with you and the children."

Abby couldn't lie to her mother, but she couldn't tell her that Kyle spent much of his time away from home.

"Where is Daddy?" Abby said changing the subject.

Judy took the hint that Abby didn't want to discuss Kyle or her marriage.

"At the Pub, he says, ' this house has lost some of its sparkle since Tabi moved to Atlanta'."

"I miss all of you too. Did Aunt Millie come home yet or is she still there?"

"She went home a few days after the wedding. I'm sure she'd love to hear from you."

"I'll call her as soon as I hang up."

Abby talked to her mother for another fifteen minutes. She put in Millie's number. The answering machine picked up.

"Hi, Aunt Millie, it's Abby. I'm calling to invite you to lunch."

Abby gave her aunt the number and hung up. It was too early to go to bed. She went into the study to get a book. Going to her room, Abby put on her nightgown and climbed into bed. She started reading. After about an hour, her eyes became heavy. She closed them for a few minutes.

Kyle stood in the doorway, his body hard with desire as he watched her sleep. Abby's dark lashes fanned her cheeks as she slept. Her hair was spread on the pillow, as she lay curled on her side. In sleep, she reached for him. If only her conscious mind would allow her the same reaction. Kyle went down to the kitchen. He heated up a bowl of soup in the microwave. He was thinking about how to get Abby to surrender her heart when he saw her note.

*Kyle:*

*"I talked to Mama tonight. She asked me to have you call her in the morning."*
*Love, Abby*

She'd signed it love, Abby. That had to mean something. An idea came to him. He would give her the best Christmas she'd ever had. He'd have to wait until morning to start his plan in motion, but it was a chance to show her he loved her.

Morning found Kyle at the office early on the phone calling Judy. When she answered, he said, "Good morning, am I calling too early?"

"Good morning, Kyle. No, you aren't calling too early." Judy answered.

"Abby left me a note saying that you wanted to speak to me."

"Yes, I want to surprise her. I'm going to make arrangements to fly to Atlanta for Christmas."

Kyle smiled. He'd also thought about sending for her family to come for Christmas.

"I'll send my plane. Tell me when you want to fly out and I'll make the arrangements."

"Christmas Eve?   Can you get her out of the house for a while that day?"

"Christmas Eve is fine.   I'll tell her I need help picking out a present for my mother.   Would she like a real family Christmas?   I can contact my parents and brother."

"She'd love it.   Abby has always loved having people around at Christmas. Would you like me to do anything?"

"No, I'll take care of everything. You just make sure you get everyone here by seven o'clock Christmas Eve. Does Abby have any favorite Christmas traditions?"

"Lights, she loves lights and an angel for the top of the tree.   We had an angel when she was a little girl. She loved that angel, but it was broken."

They discussed the rest of their plans then hung up. Kyle dialed his father's number.

"Hello, Father, what plans have you made for Christmas?" He asked.

"Kyle, my boy, good to hear from you. Same plans as always I suppose. You'll have to ask your mother." Kindred Masterson said.

"I'd like you and mother to come to my house for Christmas. I want you to meet my wife." Kyle told him.

"Your wife? Why didn't you tell us you were getting married?" Kin asked.

"It was kind of on the spur of the moment." He lied. "I'll tell you about it later. Where's Quinton?"

"Home I suppose. It is a bit early to be calling."

"Be at the house Christmas Eve by seven o'clock. We're going to have a family Christmas at our house. I have another surprise for you." Kyle hung up before his father could argue. He dialed Quinton's number.

"Cancel whatever plans you've made for Christmas. I'm having the family over this year to meet my wife." Kyle said when Quinton picked up.

"It's too early in the morning for jokes, Kyle." Quinton snapped.

"This is not a joke, little brother. Abby's family will be arriving at seven o'clock Christmas Eve. We're going to have a family Christmas this year."

"You're kidding. You actually talked a woman into marrying you?"

"Very funny. I'll explain everything some other time. Are you coming for Christmas or not?"

"I wouldn't miss this for the world, I'll be there. Do I need to bring a date?"

"No, we're only having family. I have another surprise for the family as well."

"I'll see you Christmas Eve."

Kyle hung up. He called his mother's Personal Assistant to find out where he could reach his mother. After he obtained the number, he walked to the coffee maker to warm his coffee. It would be too early to call his mother on the cruise ship. She would have already made plans for Christmas. She'd have to cancel them. A family Christmas is what Abby deserved, he would see that she got it. Kyle tried to concentrate on the paperwork on his desk, but to no avail. It was late enough to call his mother. It took so long for her to get to the phone, that by the time she finally came on the line, Kyle was ready to hang up.

"Hello, Mother, how's the cruise?" He asked.

"Not nearly as much fun as it would have been with your father." Roberta Masterson said.

"When will you be coming home?"

"The ship docks tomorrow morning."

"Would you like me to pick you up?"

"Enough social amenities, son, why are you calling?" He should have known she'd see through him.

"I'm inviting the family to my house for Christmas."

"Any special reason?"

"I want you to meet my wife."

His father could tell her about the surprise. He'd have enough hell to pay when she learned of her grandchildren.

"You're wife? Son, I think we'd better have a talk when my ship docks tomorrow." She told him where and when to pick her up.

Kyle left the office early that afternoon. He had to prepare Abby for his mother's arrival.

"Your mother is coming here? You said she was on a cruise." Abby said.

"She is, it ends tomorrow. I'm picking her up. She'll want to go home to freshen up, afterwards she'll drop by." Kyle told her.

"What time are you picking her up?"

"Ten o'clock."

Abby's mind raced. "I'll have to prepare lunch, get my hair done. Oh, I'll never be able to get it all done. Couldn't you stall her?"

"Calm down, Querida, she isn't going to bite."

Abby spent the rest of the evening preparing for her mother-in-law's visit, with help from Kyle and Agnes. Kyle had never been so nervous in his life. *I should have told mother about Kayla and Kerry. But how do you explain to your mother that you have children, when she hasn't been told anything about their mother?* He thought. When Kyle arrived to pick up his mother, she was waiting.

"Okay, son, tell me about the young lady you've chosen for your wife." Roberta demanded settling into the seat next to him.

"Her name is Abby. I met her five and a half years ago, just before I bought the house." Kyle started his story.

"You couldn't wait until I came home to get married?" "No."

"I presume there are reasons why you were so hasty. I'm very interested in finding out what they are."

"We were married in Shelby. I had to convince her to marry me so she wouldn't run away from me again."

"Run away from you again? All right, son, out with it."

"Do you remember why I bought the house?"

"Yes, to give it to the woman you planned to marry."

"What I didn't tell you was I'd met her once and never saw her again until I opened K. M. Enterprises in Shelby."

"I see."

Kyle went on to explain his relationship with Abby, leaving out the intimate details. He knew his mother would have to know about the children his affair with Abby had produced, but he couldn't tell her without revealing how he'd purposely gotten her pregnant.

# CHAPTER EIGHT

Kyle dropped his mother off at home.

"I'll just freshen up. Have Joshua pick me up in an hour."

Kyle nodded, "See you in an hour." He drove home. Abby was waiting in the living room when he walked in.

"Well?" She asked.

"Well what?" Kyle questioned back.

"You went to pick up your mother." She prompted.

"Yes?"

"And?"

"And what?"

"What did she say?"

"She'll be here in forty-five minutes. Josh is going to pick her up." Abby threw her hands up in disgust. "How did she react to our marriage?"

"She now knows everything there is to know about our relationship, except the intimacy we've shared."

"She doesn't know about Kerry and Kayla? Kyle how could you?"

He looked at her, but didn't seem to see her.

"You didn't tell her because you're ashamed."

Kyle came out of his thoughts grabbing her shoulders to shake her none too gently.

"Never, ever say that again. I am not ashamed of my children." She pulled out of his arms.

"No, only of me." She whispered softly.

"Not you, never you." He pulled her into his arms hugging her fiercely.

"I couldn't explain to my mother that I'd purposely gotten you pregnant and forced you to marry me. I want her to think we married for love, and that our children are a happy blessing as a result of that love."

"My family knows the truth." She said pulling out of his embrace.

"No, they think we married for love. Only Millie knows the truth behind your pregnancy."

"I don't understand why you're doing any of this."

"You don't have to understand now, I'll explain later. Let's just get through mother's visit."

Abby nodded her head in agreement. She went to check on Kayla and Kerry. They were asleep. Abby had already tried on several different outfits that morning. She went to her room to change clothes again. Kyle found her dressed in her bra and panties. She still carried some of the weight of her pregnancy, it only added to his desire for her.

"Mother can wait." He said crossing the room to kiss the long column of her neck.

She put her hands up to push him away, succeeding only in pulling him closer. Her defenses were stripped from her as his mouth awakened the hunger that had lain dormant. Taking little nips at his neck, Abby opened his shirt to find the hardened male nipples and bit gently. He groaned and held her to him as she aroused him further. Abby's hands traveled from his chest, down the smooth, flat line of his stomach, to his arousal. Given free rein, her hands caressed him, gently stroking, evoking ragged, uneven breaths from him. She loved Kyle as she'd longed to. Instinct led her love urged her on. He thrust her away from him, taking gulping breaths of air. At the pained look on her face, he said, "Six weeks."

Unable to comprehend, Abby stared.

"Dr. Cooper said six weeks. We have to give your body time to heal." Kyle reminded her.

Turning away from him, Abby gathered her clothes and went into the adjoining bathroom, quietly closing the door. Seeing her reflection in the mirror, she gave a strangled cry. Kyle knocked on the door.

"Abby, are you all right?"

"Yes."

He opened the door and stepped into the room. Seeing anguish in the eyes she lifted to meet his, he said, "No regrets, Querida. When we make love the time will be right for both of us. There will be no doctor's orders or arriving guests to stop me from making you my wife."

He closed the door with a thud. Roberta walked into the dining room as Abby finished setting the table for lunch.

"Where are your manners, son? Greet your mother properly." Roberta said.

Kyle rose to greet his mother.

After embracing her son, Roberta turned to Abby. "You didn't tell me how beautiful she is, Kyle." She scolded gently.

"I don't give away all my secrets, Mother." Kyle said amused.

Smiling, Roberta extended her hand to Abby, "I'm Roberta Masterson."

Abby took the warm hand in her own cool hand. Roberta gave her an affectionate squeeze.

"I'm happy to meet you, Mrs. Masterson. I'm Abby." She said.

"Mrs. Masterson? You may call me Mother, child." Roberta told her.

"Y-Yes, Mrs., Mother." Abby stammered.

"Better. Now what's this surprise your father told me about?" Roberta asked.

Abby's eyes flew to Kyle. As if on cue, Kerry and Kayla could be heard on the baby monitor.

"Babies? Do I hear babies?" Roberta asked.

"Yes." Kyle answered.

Abby was mortified that her mother-in-law had learned of her grandchildren this way. She sent Kyle an accusing glare.

"My grandchildren?" Roberta questioned.

"Yes." Kyle said.

"You have some explaining to do Kyle."

"I'll feed the children while you talk to your mother." Abby said, going to the nursery. She could be heard on the baby monitor while she was there.

"Good morning, angels." She said.

Picking up Kerry, she went to the wooden rocker and sat down.

"We'll get your belly full in no time, little man." She said, unbuttoning her blouse. Sucking noisily at her breast, Kerry pushed his fist against it. Abby laughed. "Hungry?" Kerry pushed against her breast again in answer. Abby took Kayla from her bassinet. Of the two children, Kayla most resembled her father.

"So like your daddy." Abby said wistfully.

Kayla let out a wail to let her mother know she was being neglected, not having had her turn at Abby's breast.

"Yes, I know you're hungry, Darling."

Abby placed Kayla at her breast, where she sucked greedily. She finished nursing her children and gave them their baths. Abby straightened the nursery, giving Kyle the extra time to speak with his mother. Going back into the dining room, she put on a smile that radiated bridal bliss.

"Abby, on behalf of the Mastersons, I proudly welcome you as the newest member of our family." Roberta said with a smile, pulling Abby into her warm embrace.

"Thank you, Mama." Abby said returning the hug.

Kyle smiled, noticing she had used the same endearment for his mother as she used for her own. Roberta looked at him in surprise. He shook his head to stop the question in her eyes. She would comply with his wishes...for now, but warned him there were still unanswered questions between them. Abby pulled out of Roberta's embrace, sitting down at the table, looking down into her coffee.

"When do I get to meet my grandchildren?" Roberta asked.

"I'll bring them down." Kyle answered striding off to the nursery. Roberta sat across the table from Abby.

"Abby is short for Abigail?" She asked.

"No, Tabitha." Abby answered avoiding her mother-in-law's gaze.

"A name as beautiful as its owner. You were pregnant when you married my son." Roberta stated.

At Abby's silence she charged ahead.

"Masterson men are arrogant and pigheaded. They invariably choose women like you..."

Abby's spine stiffened and her head snapped up sharply. "I beg your pardon." She said, pinning Roberta with her chocolate brown eyes.

Roberta smiled. "I wasn't insulting you Tabitha. I was explaining to you the ways of the men we love."

She held up her hand when Abby would have interrupted. "They're hard men to love. When they choose the woman they want to spend their life with, it's hard to win her love, but they do win."

Abby remembered the warning Kyle had given her. She couldn't tell Roberta that their marriage wasn't based on love, at least not on his side.

"I do love him." She confessed.

"Yes, but you're afraid of the pain that love will cause. One day when we have more time, I'll tell you the story of my courtship with Kyle's father."

"Oh, but you don't..."

"Yes, I do. Knowing the story will ease your own turmoil."

"Your grandchildren are eager to meet you Mother." Kyle said as he and Agnes brought Kayla and Kerry in.

The bassinets were set in front of Roberta. She looked into the cradles, tears forming in her eyes. "Twins. They're beautiful."

"Of course twins. What did you expect? Something wrong, Mother?" Kyle asked.

"I didn't expect... I'd given up hope..."

"I've never seen you at a loss for words, Mother." Kyle said stunned.

"Kyle!" Abby reprimanded sharply.

He looked at her, she glared back. Roberta watched the exchange, approval in her eyes. Abby picked up her son. "Would you like to meet your grandson?" She asked.

Roberta took Kerry from Abby. "What's his name?"

"Kerry Tyler." Kyle answered.

Roberta nuzzled Kerry's neck and held him for a long time.

"Would you like to hold your granddaughter?" Abby asked.

In answer Roberta gave Kerry to Kyle and received Kayla in her open arms.

"What is your name, my little angel?" She asked as she cuddled Kayla close.

"Kayla Rae, Mama." Abby answered.

Roberta held Kayla content to have the small bundle in her arms.

Both babies were sleeping contentedly. Abby and Agnes took them to the nursery.

"I like the way you've redecorated the house, Kyle." Roberta said.

"Thank you, Mother. I chose the colors because they're Abby's favorites."

Abby looked at him as she came back into the dining room, wondering why he was telling his mother such a lie. He turned away from her startled expression, choosing to look out the window. Roberta felt the tension vibrating between them. She looked from one to the other. Kyle's marriage was starting out as her own had. She had to do something.

"May I see your ring, Tabitha?" She asked.

Abby looked at her. "I'm sorry, what did you say?" Abby asked.

"I asked if I could see your wedding band." Roberta repeated.

Abby looked at her oddly. She didn't understand why a plain silver band would fascinate anyone.

"Silver bands are practical and highly visible." She said, pointedly looking at Kyle's left hand. He looked at the silver band Abby had placed on his finger on their wedding day.

"And warm." Abby whispered, studying her own wedding band. Roberta was getting exasperated with them. She stood to go.

"I'm leaving. Kyle walk me to the car." She ordered.

Surprised by her tone, he obeyed. They stood next to the car. "Don't let your pride cloud your good judgment, Kyle. I almost ruined my marriage to your father because I was too proud." Roberta told him.

"My pride doesn't have anything to do with this, Mother. Abby doesn't trust me. She wouldn't have married me if I hadn't threatened a custody battle." Kyle admitted unexpectedly, unable to lie to her.

"You threatened her?" Roberta said shocked.

He'd gone this far, he might as well tell her the rest. "Yes, and the pregnancy wasn't an accident." He told her.

This time he hadn't shocked her.

"Kyle how could you do such a thing? No, don't tell me, you are your father's son."

Kyle laughed at himself. "I may be my father's son, but I can't force Abby to love me, Mother. I spent five years searching for her. And since finding her I've tried to convince her we belong together."

"You can't convince her if she refuses to listen. Show her, I know from living with your father for all of these years that you inherited more than a fair amount of persuasiveness."

Roberta climbed into the car and let Joshua know she was ready to go, leaving Kyle standing in the driveway. He stood staring after her for a few moments then went into the house.

"Abby." He said.

"In the kitchen." She answered.

Kyle walked to the kitchen. He found Abby putting away lunch after making coffee.

"We didn't get around to eating lunch." She said unnecessarily.

"What plans have you made for Christmas?" He asked.

"I'm surprised you're bothering to ask. You're rarely home. I assumed you'd have made plans of your own as usual." Abby snapped.

"I wouldn't miss the twins' first Christmas." He told her harshly.

"I'd rather you not call them the twins. They do have names." She said, slamming coffee down in front of him. The contents spilled over onto her hand. She cried out as the hot liquid burned her.

Kyle got out of his seat. "Let me see." He commanded.

"Don't touch me." Abby spat.

"I have to see how badly it's burned." He said.

"I can take care of it myself." She informed him.

"Don't be stubborn. Let me look at it." He insisted.

Abby shoved her hand at him. He looked at it and led her to the sink. He turned on the water and held her hand under the cold water.

"How does it feel?" He asked.

"It's fine. You can let go now." Abby said.

"We're going to spend Christmas at home, together. Agnes will be going to her sister's for the holidays. I'd like you to help me pick out a present for my mother. We'll be leaving early Christmas Eve morning. Agnes can watch the children." Kyle said and walked to his study.

Abby began spluttering about the arrogance of the male species. Deciding she'd had enough of taking orders from Kyle, she followed him, her brown eyes shooting sparks.

"How dare you expect me to change my plans at the last minute? Did you bother asking if I'd go shopping with you? No, not the great Kyle Masterson. He gives orders and expects everyone to obey. Well forget it, I no longer take orders from you." She said slapping her hand on his desk, knocking several papers off.

Kyle walked around the desk so it wouldn't be between them. "I never claimed to be "the great" anything. You're my wife, I expect you to help choose the gift we'll be giving to my mother." Kyle told her, losing his temper.

"You expect? Damn you and your arrogance." She said defiantly. Abby realized she'd gone too far when his eyes became dangerous gray slits. He pulled her to him and kissed her savagely. Thrusting his tongue into her mouth, he kissed her without abandon. She pushed her hands into his hair and kissed him, allowing her tongue to dance with his. He groaned and laid her across the desk knocking off several more papers. Abby thighs parted against the thrust of his arousal, she welcomed the invasion, willing him to make love to her.

Kyle trailed hot kisses down the column of her throat. When he came to her blouse he ripped the buttons open with his teeth. Her breasts were cradled in a practical nursing bra. He sucked greedily at them; she arched into him, relishing the sweet pain.

"Kyle, I want you." She was forced to admit.

"I want to make love to you, Querida." He said, passion evident in his voice.

Querida...the word he'd told her meant mistress. She remembered the perfume and lipstick on his clothes. Abby broke away from him.

"Where are you going?" He asked.

"Anywhere to get away from you." She snapped.

"I want an explanation, Abby." He commanded.

"Explanation for what?" She hedged.

"Why you won't let go of your feelings." He growled.

"You haven't given me any reason to, Kyle. Since I've been home, you haven't spent much time with the children or me. I won't be one of your playmates. You've made it clear each of us will lead our own lives." She told him and walked away.

Kyle went after her. When he caught up with her he pulled her around to face him.

"And if I told you I want us to lead our lives together?"

"If you did, you wouldn't spend so much time away from home. I've smelled the perfume and seen the lipstick on your clothes. Do you think I'm blind or just stupid?"

"I haven't been unfaithful to you Abby. I need companionship." He told her desperately.

"I don't believe you've been unfaithful in the true sense of the word. And I don't care how many companions you have, but I would appreciate your discretion in the future."

Christmas Eve morning Abby was up early to go shopping with Kyle. She had no reason to vent her anger at Roberta just because her son was a... The right word still hadn't come after their confrontation two days ago.

"You have my cell phone number and my pager number. We'll be home after supper." Kyle told Agnes as he pushed Abby out the door.

"You don't have to worry about a thing, Mr. Masterson. I'll take care of things while you're gone." Agnes assured him.

Kyle urged Abby into the car.

"Where's the fire, Kyle?" She asked breathless.

"Fire?" He repeated.

"You've been rushing me around all morning. If I hadn't insisted on nursing Kerry and Kayla this morning you'd have let Agnes give them formula."

"We have a lot to do and I want to get an early start."

He had rushed her out of the house so she wouldn't see the crew coming to put up the light displays he'd planned. He could have put up the lights himself, but wouldn't have had the day to spend with Abby.

He dragged her through every one of the shops, insisting on looking at everything they had.

Kyle asked Abby her opinions on the gifts he chose. He picked out a case of Scotch for Andrew. She told him it was suitable. When he'd picked out panties for Andie, he was teasing. Abby told him they weren't wild enough. He proceeded to find and hold up wilder and wilder colors. Abby enjoyed watching him search through the piles to find the matching bras to the panties he'd selected. She had tears in her eyes from laughter by the time he emerged with a dozen of each. For Eric, Abby suggested a briefcase to go with his new position at K. M. Enterprises. Kyle asked if it should be in a wild color too. Abby doubled over in laughter. He looked perplexed. She looked at his frown, realizing he was serious.

"No, conservative will do. Andie is the only wildflower in our bunch. She takes a little after Nana Phillips."

Abby picked out several wind chimes for Judy, knowing her mother would love to hear their music when the breeze caught them. Samuel would be getting pipes and tobacco.

"What do you think Millie would like?" Kyle asked.

"Something romantic. She loves romance." Abby told him.

After searching, Abby found a crystal paperweight in the shape of a heart. It would cast rainbows in the sun's rays.

Packing everything into the trunk of the Corvette, Kyle took Abby to lunch. At the table he looked through the choices on the menu.

"Pancakes, three eggs over easy, sausage and coffee." He told the waitress.

"Chef's salad with ranch dressing and a Diet Coke." Abby said. The waitress left to fill their order.

"You aren't on a diet, are you?" Kyle asked.

Abby looked at him, stung by the question. "No." She answered.

"Why the salad for lunch?"

"I like salad. If I don't have to chop, slice and dice, I like it even more."

Kyle laughed. "Well don't try living on it. I'd hate to see those curves disappear." He looked her over appreciatively.

Abby blushed, and took a drink of her water, hoping to erase the heat from her face. While they ate Kyle asked Abby for suggestions on gifts for his family. She reminded him she hadn't met his father or brother. Tossing out ideas, he went from serious to funny, to just plain ludicrous.

He cut the white part away from his eggs. All that remained were the yolks. Abby was still laughing over his latest suggestion when he attacked the yolk with his fork. Opening his mouth he put it in and closed it, letting the slimy fluid run down his throat. Abby grimaced at the sight. Kyle smiled at the face she made. When he finished swallowing the yolk, he said, "I like the yolk." Abby shuddered in distaste. He attacked the second yolk with his fork picking it up and putting it in his mouth allowing it to slide down his throat. Abby shuddered again. When he turned to the third egg Abby ignored him.

Lunch finished, Kyle took Abby to a bookstore where they found a book for his father. Quinton proved to be harder to choose for. Kyle told Abby of Quinton's love of working with wood. She suggested a gift certificate from a lumberyard. That way they wouldn't choose the wrong materials for his projects.

There was only Roberta to get a gift for. Kyle deliberately made the shopping almost impossible. Every gift Abby chose was picked apart until she wanted to throw it at him. She'd been trying to find a gift for two hours.

"You're being stubborn, Kyle. Every one of the gifts I've chosen has been appropriate. If I didn't know better I'd think you were being deliberately finicky."

"You've chosen elaborate and exquisite gifts. Mother isn't like any of those things."

"You want me to choose a gift I'd get for Mama?"

"Yes, Mother will see the love and care you've used to choose her gift."

Abby hadn't thought of it that way. "What would I pick for Mama?" She thought. She knew what she was looking for, but finding it was the problem. With renewed energy she dragged Kyle from the shop. For over an hour she took him from one shop to another. Coming to a shop displaying stained glass, she pulled him in.

"Sun catchers?"

She looked at him indignantly. "They are not sun catchers. This is stained glass. Very ordinary, very down to earth, very Mama."

Going through the shop she chose a picture frame with pink hues, a night light of indistinct reds, and a picture of twins joined by a heart; Kyle's sun catcher, for the window, in multi-shades of blue.

"I'm starved." Abby said after they'd carefully placed the gifts in the trunk.

She had bought gifts for Kyle and her children when she'd been shopping the week before. They were wrapped and under the tree at home.

"I have one more stop to make. Go back to the car and decide where you want to go for supper, I'll catch up." Kyle told her then kissed her. Abby nodded and went back to the car. Kyle's kiss had tasted of pure joy and contentment.

He walked back to the car with a little boy grin on his face that said, "I know something you don't." His hands were empty and his grin was infectious.

"Did you decide where you want to go for supper?" He asked.

"Yes." Abby answered.

Eating a leisurely supper, comfortable in each other's company, they displayed their love to the world. Not until later would Abby see the day as Kyle had intended it. She was tired. Laying her head against the seat, she relaxed and let the day seep warmly through her. Kyle turned into the driveway; she sat forward in delight.

"Look Kyle, look. Aren't they beautiful." She exclaimed.

On the house and in the yard, thousands of lights twinkled at them. When Kyle parked the car Abby jumped out and went to each display of lights. A lighted snowman stood in the front yard. Electric lighted candles stood sentinel on either side of the door. Trees and bushes were alight with color. Santa's house was close to the road. A light lined fence ran up to it, inside glowed with more lights. Looking at the house, Abby saw it had been lined with lights of various colors. On the roof was Santa's sleigh, where he sat. Pulling the sleigh were eight reindeer, out front was Rudolph and his shiny red nose. In her exuberance, Abby threw her arms around Kyle's neck, knocking him down. Falling, he caught her in his arms and returned the affection in the way she had given it. He lay on the cold, wet ground absorbing the feelings erupting from her.

His hands traveled lazily from her back to her bottom. He made clear the desire springing to life. She wriggled against him playfully. They played like children in the snow.

"Are you going to play in the snow all night?" Kin asked affectionately.

Abby lay atop Kyle, she tried to get up, he held her to him.

"Hello, Father nice evening." Kyle answered, looking toward the direction his father's voice had come from.

"Yes, if you would let go of the young woman in your arms, we would like to make her acquaintance." Kin told him.

Kyle released his hold on Abby, then stood up and pulled her to her feet.

"Father, my wife, Tabitha. Abby, my father, Kindred." He introduced.

Kin took Abby's hand in his.

"Too good for the likes of you, Kyle my boy." Kin said looking at Abby.

"I'll take that as a compliment." Kyle said as he ushered them inside the house.

A chorus of surprise rang out as they entered the living room. Abby's eyes sparkled and tears came into them when she saw her family. Kyle had brought Christmas to her. Turning to him, her eyes shone with love when she looked up at him.

"Merry Christmas, Love." Kyle whispered as he bent his head to kiss her.

She wrapped her arms around his waist and took pleasure in his kiss. "Twice I have to remind you of your duties as host." Kin complained, mock sternness in his voice.

Kyle broke the kiss. Chuckling, he said, "Having a beautiful woman in my arms takes precedence over duties, Father."

Turning Abby in his arms he made the necessary introductions.

Their families had been getting acquainted while Abby and Kyle were out. Excusing themselves, Kyle and Abby went to change into dry clothes.

Kyle joined the party downstairs while Abby checked on Kayla and Kerry. She nursed and bathed them. Having spent time with her children, she went to join their guests. Going into the living room, she saw everyone except Andrea. Wondering where she had gone, Abby went to look for her. Finding her in the dining room, Abby saw the tense set of her shoulders.

"Andie, are you okay?" She asked.

Andrea turned haunted emerald eyes toward Abby.

Abby went to her sister, kneeling before her chair. "Andrea, what is it? Tell me, please. You're scaring me." Abby beseeched.

"You tried to tell me, but I didn't understand. I can't go out there, Abby. I just can't." Andrea wailed softly.

"Andie, I don't understand. What did I tell you? Have I hurt you in some way?" Abby asked.

Not for anything in the world would she hurt Andrea.

"So like Kyle, yet different. I can't explain it. He's Kyle's brother. He makes me feel..." Andrea trailed off.

"Quinton? What has he done? Damn it Andrea, talk to me." Abby stood up, grabbing her by the shoulders, shaking her.

"If he's done something we'll talk to Kyle. He'll be able to straighten him out." Abby said.

Andrea came back to herself again. Realizing Abby was still holding onto her, she said, "Forgive me Abby. I don't know what got into me.

I'm fine now."

Abby released her. The haunted look was gone it was replaced by sadness, reservation.

"There you two are. We're opening the champagne." Kyle said slipping his arms around Abby.

"We were taking a break from all of the excitement." Abby told him.

"Champagne sounds wonderful." Andrea said too brightly.

Champagne was passed around. Abby refused the glass offered to her, using the excuse that she was nursing. Andrea drank her champagne and added Abby's to it.

The party continued into the early morning.

# CHAPTER NINE

Christmas morning Abby was up early with Kayla and Kerry. After nursing them, she watched them sleep thanking God for the many blessings he'd given her. Silently she went to the kitchen to start Christmas dinner. She found her mother and Roberta in the kitchen drinking coffee.

"Good morning, Mama." She said.

"Good morning, Abby."

"Good morning, Tabitha." Judy and Roberta said in unison.

Abby poured herself a cup of coffee, added milk, and then joined them at the counter.

"Your granddaddy sends his love and wishes you a Merry Christmas." Judy said.

"I wish he could have made the trip." Abby answered.

"He offered to take over the Pub while your father took his first real vacation in twenty years. Andrew couldn't turn him down." Judy explained.

"I'm just glad you're all here." Abby said hugging her mother.

Kyle stumbled into the kitchen. "Good morning, any coffee?" He asked as he bent to kiss Abby. He took a drink of her milk-laced coffee. "How can you drink that stuff?" Grimacing he went to pour himself a cup of black coffee. Taking a drink he sighed. "Now that's coffee." Like the coffee, he was wild, strong and untamed.

"Something smells good. Did you two stay up all night making dinner?" Abby asked, turning to her mother and mother-in-law.

"Not all night. We did get a few hours' sleep." Roberta defended.

"You shouldn't have gotten up to make dinner. I could have done it." Abby told them.

"Now Abby, calm down. Cooking for a large group of people isn't easy. We wanted to help." Judy said.

Before Abby could answer Kyle put his arm around her waist urging her out of the kitchen. "I have something I want to give you." He said guiding her toward the stairs and up to their room. Going to his dresser, he opened the top drawer, withdrawing a small box. Walking to Abby, he handed it to her. Hesitating, she took the box. Looking into his clear blue eyes, she asked, "What's this?"

"My Christmas present to you. Open it." He answered.

Glancing at the box, she slowly opened the lid. There lay on a bed of velvet, the most perfect one carat oval opal surrounded by a quarter carat of diamonds. She stared at the ring. The opal was her favorite gem.

"As far back as anyone can remember, all Masterson brides have worn their favorite gem as the center of their engagement ring." Kyle explained.

She looked at him, tears in her eyes at his thought of...*What word was she looking for? Love?*

"Would you like me to put it on for you?" He asked.

Wordlessly she nodded, watching as he took the ring out of the box. Taking her left hand in his, he put the ring on her finger, kissing the back of her hand. When she raised her head he looked into her eyes. Bending his head, he kissed her long and sensuously.

"Merry Christmas, Mrs. Masterson." He said huskily.

"Merry Christmas, Kyle." She said breathless.

He pulled her to him, locked his hands at her waist and held her.

"Thank you, Kyle. It's the most beautiful ring I've ever seen." She stepped up on tiptoe to kiss his cheek. He moved his head slightly to get the full affect of her kiss. Instead of the chaste kiss she'd intended, it was sensuous and intoxicating.

Tearing his mouth from hers, he set her away from him. "I'm not made of stone, Sweetheart. Making love to you is foremost on my mind, doctor's orders last." He said to a surprised Abby. She blushed.

"You're beautiful when you blush, Querida."

He went to take a cold shower. Abby gathered her clothes and straightened their room while she waited her turn in the shower. After her shower she dressed in white jeans and one of Kyle's shirts, tucked into the jeans, leaving the top buttons undone. She chose not to wear socks. Kyle raked her outfit with desire burning in his eyes. The jeans hugged her curves lovingly. She looked sexy wearing his shirt, even sexier with the buttons undone. When he came to her feet, he chuckled, "No socks, Querida?"

"I don't like shoes and socks." She answered.

Kyle was dressed in muscle hugging jeans and a sweater. He also wore loafers without socks. They went down to see if breakfast was ready. Everyone, except Andrea and Quinton were in the dining room. Millie had gone home after the party had ended early that morning.

Abby wasn't surprised that Andie hadn't come out of her room yet. She'd drunk quite a bit of champagne the night before.

"I heard my grandchildren earlier. Are they awake?" Kin asked.

"No, they went back to sleep after breakfast." Abby told him. "Son, we need to have a talk about propriety." Kin told Kyle. "Yes, sir." Kyle mumbled into his coffee.

Breakfast over Kin motioned Kyle into the study.

"All right, son, explain why I found your mother in tears the day she came home from her cruise." Kin demanded.

*"Where shall I start? The night I met Abby, the day I found her, the night she became pregnant, when I learned she was pregnant?"* Kyle asked self-derisively.

"That's enough, Kyle. Self-reproach will only serve to make matters worse. Suppose you start at the beginning." Kin urged patiently.

"I met Abby about six months before I bought the house. The same night I met her, she disappeared. I searched Atlanta for two days trying to find her." Kyle began.

"You didn't find her."

"No."

"That was about the time you started pushing yourself like the devil was after you."

"Yes, I tried to drive her out of my mind."

"It didn't work?"

"No, she invaded my days as well as my nights. I'd finally convinced myself, or thought I had, that she didn't exist."

Kyle began to pace restlessly, running his fingers through his hair.

"I went to Shelby with my new division manager. Imagine my surprise when I met his sister."

"Abby?"

Kyle nodded. "Isn't it funny? The woman I'd tried so hard to convince myself didn't exist was standing there defiantly telling me to go to hell with her eyes."

Reading more into what his son had told him, Kin said, "How did you expect her to react?"

"I didn't expect icy disdain. My God, on the night we met." Kyle stated.

Kin grinned. "Son, you have a lot to learn about women."

"I'm well aware of that, Father. I fully expected to take up where we'd left off."

"And she was having none of it."

"Right. She informed me that she didn't want anything to do with me."

"And like a true Masterson, you thought you could convince her otherwise."

"Right again. She ran away from me again."

"Before or after you'd uh... planned her pregnancy."

"After." Kyle stopped, looking in amazement at his father. "How did you know?"

"I did the same thing to your mother. Unfortunately she miscarried."

So that was what his mother had meant when she'd told him he was his father's son.

"Anyway, I found her again here in Atlanta, living with her aunt. I still had the Shelby Division to complete and couldn't be with her. I called her aunt frequently to check on her."

Kyle ceased his pacing.

"She didn't know you were talking to her aunt."

"No. If she had, she'd have gone through the roof. After I found her again, her aunt invited me to supper. That's when I learned she was pregnant and told her I'd planned it."

"She was less than, shall we say, joyful."

"Yeah. She threw me out of the house. Millie and I schemed to get her to Shelby."

"When she did get there she wasn't exactly thrilled that she'd been double-crossed."

"Uh huh. She threatened to come back to Atlanta. Then she was kidnapped by her former fiancée. When she was back home I uh, convinced her it would be in her best interest to marry me."

"You threatened her."

Kyle looked bewildered at his father. "Who's telling this story, you or me? Yesterday, spending the day together was the first sign we could have a normal marriage."

"Which brings us back to where we started. Why didn't you contact us when Abby agreed to marry you?"

"I was afraid she would change her mind."

"And the children?"

"I hadn't thought of how to tell you about them without sacrificing my pride."

"When you fall in love pride always takes a fall."

"Not exactly words of wisdom, Father."

"No, but a word of advice. In the future, when you plan your wife's pregnancies, I suggest you let her in on your plans." Kin told him and walked out the door.

Abby was helping in the kitchen while Kyle and Kin talked in the study. Andrea stumbled in, her eyes red and swollen.

Abby dragged her into the study. "All right, spill it." She demanded.

"What?" Andie asked.

"Why I found you in the dining room last night, why you drank too much champagne and why you look like hell." Abby told her.

"It's nothing. I overreacted. Must be the holidays making me sentimental." Andie answered.

"Andie, I know you better than anybody, remember. We've virtually been joined at the hip since birth. What happened with Quinton?"

"It's none of your business. I told you I overreacted."

Andie opened the door and stormed out. Running into Kyle, she walked around him.

"What's the matter with Andie?" He asked.

"You and Quinton don't know when to quit do you?  First me, now Andie! You just have to win no matter who it hurts." Abby accused as she watched Quinton come down the hall toward them. She left them standing in the hallway.

Quinton stopped behind Kyle.  "What was that all about?" He asked.

"Damned if I know." Kyle muttered.

Brother looked at brother, deciding that women, Phillips women to be precise, confused the hell out of them.

Christmas Dinner was festive. Kerry and Kayla were brought to the dining room to join in the festivity. Agnes had left that morning to go to her sister's.  Kyle sat at the head of the table, Abby sat at the opposite end. Everyone complimented Judy and Roberta on the wonderful dinner.

Kyle ate and joined in the lively conversation while stealing glances at his wife. When he managed to make eye contact with her, she glared at him with contempt. *How had they gone from warm companionship to cold contempt?* He wished he'd never forced her into marriage.  His blood pressure was rising by the second. *What had Andrea told her to make Abby hate him?*

No one seemed to notice the icy glares Abby sent him. She pretended the dinner she forced herself to eat, didn't taste like cardboard. She was a fool to believe Kyle had enjoyed her company yesterday. He had shown her again, that she was a possession to be used and discarded when he saw fit. Abby and Andrea insisted on clearing up after dinner.

"Are you going to tell me what happened last night?" Abby demanded when she and Andrea were alone in the dining room.

"Abby I told you... "Andie began.

"I'm not blind, Andrea. I saw the look in your eyes when I came in. It was haunted." Abby shot at her.

"More like hunted." Andie murmured.

"If you won't tell me what's going on between you, I'll ask Quinton."

"Don't you dare, I won't let you interfere. I can take care of myself."

"You may be able to stop my interference, but what about the rest of the family?"

"They wouldn't."

"They would and did."

"Well, hell."

"Precisely."

They drew out the cleaning up, Abby made a fresh pot of coffee.

"I've made fresh coffee. It'll be ready in about ten minutes." She announced walking into the living room. She sat next to the fireplace.

"Shall we open the gifts?"

She walked over to the tree as she spoke. Sorting out the gifts, she passed each one to its owner. Paper was torn, boxes were opened.

Andrew expressed gratitude for the Scotch. Andrea's face suffused with color when she pulled the underwear out of the box Abby had packed it in. Quinton sat next to Andrea. He grabbed at the box when she shoved the underwear back in.

"What's in the box, Andrea? We didn't get to see what's inside." He teased.

"Undergarments." She muttered softly.

"What? I didn't hear you?" He demanded.

"Quinton!" Roberta said sternly.

"Yes, Mother?" He said.

"You're embarrassing her." Roberta reprimanded.

He looked at Andrea's down bent head. Her hair hid her face from his view.

"I apologize for embarrassing you, Andrea." He said.

"Apology accepted." Andrea said lifting her head to meet his gaze.

His eyes burned with desire when he looked at her. She quickly looked away. Eric voiced his appreciation for the briefcase. Judy held up the wind chimes and smiled at the music they played. Millie fell in love with the crystal paperweight. Kin acknowledged the book, saying it was one he had been wanting. Quinton was delighted with the gift certificate. He now had time to start a new project.

Roberta thanked Abby for the beautiful stained glass she'd chosen. When Abby started to deny she'd picked it out, Roberta told her Kyle thought of it just as something to catch the sun.

"I see Kyle has kept the Masterson Bride Tradition." Roberta said, looking at Abby's engagement ring.

Abby looked at her. "I'm sorry, what did you say?" She asked.

"I'm glad Kyle didn't give you a diamond engagement ring." Roberta told her.

Abby looked at her left hand. "Oh, yes. I've always liked opals, their warm and full of fire." Abby said.

"Just as you are." Kyle muttered to himself.

Abby heard him. Turning her head, she gazed at him.

He lifted a brow at her. Abby's engagement ring was admired when she displayed it.

"It's beautiful, Kyle. Wherever did you find it?" Roberta asked.

He gave a shrug of his shoulders and said, "I had it custom-made for my bride."

Abby tried to ignore the warmth in his voice. She had to remind herself he was very good at pretense. When Kyle unwrapped the sweater Abby had made for him he showed pleasant surprise. It was a mixture of the blue and gray in his eyes. He hadn't known she could crochet anything other than the ornaments she'd made for the tree. Excusing himself, he went to put it on. Coming back into the room, he showed her how well it fit. It emphasized his broad chest and flat stomach, and the sleeves molded his arms. Abby had done well with her measurements. Paper and boxes were cleared away and put into the trash.

Abby went into the kitchen to get the coffee she'd made. Taking it into the living room, she poured it into cups. Passing the cups as she filled them, she said, "Would anyone like dessert to go with their coffee?"

No one was ready for dessert. Millie gave her thanks for the lovely gifts, made her good-byes and went home. Kerry and Kayla began to fuss for their dinner. Abby began unbuttoning the shirt she wore.

"What are you doing?" Kyle hissed.

"Nursing." She answered.

"Not down here you're not." He told her harshly.

"Kyle, it's perfectly natural and acceptable for a woman to nurse in public." Roberta told him.

"I will not have my wife undressing in public." Kyle said sternly.

He helped Abby take Kayla and Kerry to the nursery so she could nurse them. Expecting him to go downstairs, Abby finished unbuttoning her blouse. She stopped when he closed the door, remaining in the nursery.

"Don't let my presence disrupt your nursing." He told her.

"I'd rather be alone." She answered sharply.

"I want to know what Andrea said to you this morning."

"I don't want to discuss it."

"I do! I'm not leaving until you tell me why you've gone back to doubting our relationship."

She picked up a blanket and prepared to nurse her children. Settling in the rocker, she began to nurse.

"I was a fool to trust you. Yesterday, spending the day together was a cleverly hidden disguise. You wanted me to believe I could trust you, I did." She said.

Kyle was trembling with the force of his anger. "What was my reason for making you believe you could trust me?" He asked.

"I have no idea." She snapped at him.

"When you think you've found a solution, you know where to find me." He said.

~ 190 ~

Opening the door, he walked out, slamming it. He went to the study, slamming the door behind him after walking inside. Quinton went in search of Kyle. Coming to the study, he knocked on the door.

"Come in." Kyle called gruffly.

Quinton opened the door and stepped in. "Trouble in paradise, big brother?" He guessed.

"Paradise? Hell is paradise compared to my life right now." Kyle snapped.

"Want to talk about it?" Quinton asked.

"Thanks, but no. Do you have any idea what Abby was talking about this morning?"

"In the hall when I came out of my room?" At Kyle's nod, "Not a clue."

"She said you and I don't know when to quit; first her then Andrea. If you hurt Andrea, you hurt Abby and vice versa." Kyle said thoughtfully.

"That's it! You did something to upset Andrea. As close as those two are, you've upset Abby as well."

"Excuse me, I met Andrea last night. How could I have upset her in that short period of time?"

"What happened?"

Color ran into Quinton's face. "Nothing."

"The color in your face suggests otherwise, little brother."

Quinton threw his brother a look that told him he was treading in dangerous territory.

"Another Masterson takes the plunge into the wonderful world of romance." Kyle remarked sardonically.

"They are twins. And...we've always had similar, slightly different tastes in women." Quinton defended.

"Little brother, we're riding the same roller coaster. Ride together and we may just survive those twins of ours."

Kyle walked out of the study. Going to the living room, he spotted Andrea sitting on the porch swing. He joined her. "Want to talk about it?" He asked, sitting next to her.

Andrea shrugged. "There's nothing to talk about." She told him.

"Abby thinks there is. She said..."

Kyle let the rest of his words go unspoken.

Andie swung around. "What did she say? I told her not to interfere!" She said hotly.

"Relax, Andie. She hasn't said anything. I was just wondering what you said to her. This morning she implied Quint might have done something to hurt you."

"That's silly! I only met Quinton last night for crying out loud." She jumped up going into the house to find Abby.

In her search, she ran smack into Quint. He put his hands on her shoulders to steady her. "Whoa, slow down Little One. Where's the fire?" He said. Electricity from his touch shot through Andrea. He felt the heat generated from touching her.

"Let go of me!" She said through clenched teeth.

He let go and held up his hands in mock surrender. "What did you tell Abby?" He asked harshly.

"I didn't tell Abby anything!" She snapped.

Quinton lifted his eyebrow in challenge. "No? Then suppose you tell me why she's biting Kyle's head off."

"I don't understand."

"Neither do I, but because of the 'nothing' you told her, she thinks I've done something to hurt you."

"What? I have to talk to Abby." Andie made to go around him. He put his hands on her arms to stop her.

"Hold on a minute. Talking isn't going to help. I suggest an alternate plan."

"Such as?"

"We, you and I, show her there is no discord between us."

"How do you propose we do that?"

"We go out... together. Double date."

"And you think that will work?"

"We won't know if we don't try. New Year's Eve?"

"For Abby I'll do anything."

"In the meantime I suggest we pretend we enjoy one another's company." Quinton bent his head and kissed her.

"Agreed." Andrea said, trembling from the impact of his kiss.

New Year's Eve Abby and Andrea were dressing for their double date. Roberta was looking after Kerry and Kayla.

"Andie, how does this dress look?" Abby asked.

Andrea turned around to look at her.  "It's beautiful."  At Abby's skeptical frown she added,

"Abby, the weight you gained with Kayla and Kerry isn't going to disappear overnight."

"I know. It's just that... well... my hips look... huge."

"You're imagining things. Now hurry, or we're going to be late."

As Kyle helped her out of the car, Abby noticed the name of the club. It was the one she'd met Kyle at five and a half years before. She looked at him, "Accident or intentional?" She asked.

"Intentional." He answered.

"Why?" She whispered softly.

"I was hoping to start over where we began." He stated honestly.

"I can't make promises, but I am willing to try."

He smiled. "That's all I ask. Let's go woman, the sooner we get this date started, the sooner I can take you home."

When they went inside they saw that Quinton and Andrea had found a table. When they sat down, a waiter appeared.

"What can I get you?" Tom asked. "Hi, Kyle. You haven't been in for a while."

"I've been busy. This is my wife Tabitha, her sister Andrea, and you know Quint." Kyle said.

Tom acknowledged the introductions by nodding his head. His gaze lingered on Andrea. She blushed a becoming shade of pink. Kyle noticed the murderous glint in his brother's eyes.

"I'll have Scotch. Abby?" He said.

"Diet Coke." Abby responded.

Startled out of his assessment of Andrea, Tom said, "Huh, oh sure thing. What can I get you?"

"Strawberry Daiquiri." Andrea said.

"Scotch. Make it a double." Quinton ordered.

Tom took a step back, confused by Quinton's violent tone. "Sure thing. Coming right up." He said.

He walked off to get their drinks. Kyle stood and extended his hand to Abby.

"May I have this dance, madam?" He said bowing.

Smiling, Abby put her hand in his, "You may sir." She answered.

He led her to the dance floor pulling her into his arms. Dancing with him, Abby felt the return of feelings they'd shared that night so long ago. Even though time had passed, their bodies remembered the steps as they let the world fade away.

"The music has stopped, Love. Unless you want me to make love to you on the dance floor, I suggest we go back to our table." Kyle told her.

Abby blushed a pretty shade of red and let him lead her back to the table. Another song started.

"Would you like to dance, Miss Phillips?" Quinton asked tersely for only Andrea's ears.

"Don't feel you have to entertain me, Mr. Masterson. I'm quite happy where I am." Andrea hissed.

"We're supposed to make Abby believe we don't hate each other, remember." He snapped.

Andrea placed her hand in his. "For Abby." She whispered.

They made a great show of pretending they enjoyed being in one another's company. Tom brought their drinks. A blonde followed along, bringing champagne. She sauntered over to Kyle, planting a loud kiss on his cheek, she said, "I hear you've given up your freedom, boss."

"Afraid so, Iris. How are things going?" Kyle said.

"Look around you." She said, putting the champagne in the middle of the table.

Someone yelled for her, with a wave of her hand she was gone. Tom took the money Kyle held out to him, handed him the change and was gone.

"Did I hear that woman call you boss?" Abby asked incredulously.

"Mm hm." Kyle answered sipping his Scotch.

"You own this club?" She said, taking a drink of her Diet Coke.

"No, you do." He told her.

Abby began choking and coughing at Kyle's statement. He patted her on the back until she was breathing normally.

"I beg your pardon." She said.

"I said you own..."

"I heard what you said. How?"

"The day we were married the club was turned over to you. Legally it still belongs to me. As soon as you sign the ownership papers it becomes yours to do with as you wish."

"Why?"

"I think you know why." He regarded her steadily.

Abby's eyes became the melted chocolate he loved. He'd bought the club hoping his raven-haired love would one day walk in to claim the heart she'd stolen. Now he knew she was willing to try giving hers into his loving care. Abby put her hands on either side of his smooth face. Drawing his mouth to within an inch of her own, she said, "Thank you, my Love." She kissed him. The kiss was soft and fleeting, but a wealth of feeling was shot into it.

"Hello, earth to Abby." Andrea said, tapping her on the shoulder.

"What?" Abby asked.

"I asked if I could borrow Kyle for this dance." Andie repeated. Abby smiled as she recognized the Janie Fricke song, 'He's A Heartache (Looking For A Place To Happen.')

Her knowing gaze swept to Andrea. "Of course." Andie hastily pulled Kyle to the dance floor.

"Something you want to tell me, Andie?" Kyle asked laughing.

"Nope." She answered.

"Sure?"

"Positive."

Kyle laughed again as he whirled Andie across the crowded dance floor.

"You're a puzzle, dear sister-in-law. Quint loves to solve puzzles."

"Shut up, Kyle."

Quinton dragged Abby onto the dance floor.

She found herself roughly shoved into her husband's arms as Quinton traded places with him. Winded, she turned startled brown eyes to meet Kyle's laughing blue ones.

"What just... Never mind, I don't want to know." Abby said.

"What were you going to say?" Kyle asked.

"Forget it."

"Are you sure?"

"Absolutely positive."

"Ah, Sweetheart, you are a mystery. I've always loved a good mystery."

Moving his hands to her hips, he pulled her closer. She laid her cheek against his chest. His heart beat wildly. Smiling, she let the music flow around her. As the song ended they made their way back to the table.

"Where's Andie?" Abby asked Quinton looking around the club.

"Hiding." He muttered to himself.

Draining his glass in one swallow, he signaled for another. "When does your family plan to go back to Shelby?" He asked.

"Tomorrow afternoon." Abby answered.

"Tomorrow?" Quinton repeated, taken aback.

"Mm. Daddy has to get back to the Pub and Andie has to get back to work." Abby said absently, still looking for Andrea.

Spotting her at the bar, she walked to her. "Are you all right?" She asked.

"Yes, fine. I'm hungry. Can I bring you anything?" Andie asked. Abby read the menu behind the bar.

"Cheeseburger, catsup and mustard, onion rings, and another Diet Coke." She said.

Andie nodded, and said, "I'll give the order to the bartender and have it sent to our table."

Abby nodded and went back to the table. Andie wandered back to the table after ordering their food. "The food will be here in about twenty minutes." She stated.

When the food arrived Abby picked up an onion ring to put into her mouth. Kyle took her hand, guiding it to his mouth. Putting half the onion ring into his mouth, he pulled Abby closer. Prompting her to open her mouth, he put the other half in. Obediently she ate her half. He repeated the process with the remaining onion rings. When he came to the cheeseburger, he tore off bites, feeding them to her.

"Just like a baby bird. Put food in front of you and you open your mouth." He teased.

"Oh yeah." She said, taking the sandwich from him. Tearing off a piece, she pretended to feed him in the same manner he'd used to feed her. He opened his mouth to take the bite she offered. She popped it into her mouth, eyes sparkling. She tore off another piece, repeating the game.

She was surprised when his hand snaked out and he put it into his mouth. Gently suckling her fingers, he coaxed her to continue the game. When the last of the cheeseburger had been eaten, he urged her to the dance floor. He'd gotten deeply aroused, as they'd played their game with the food.

He pressed against her to show her how their enjoyment of the food had affected him. During the rest of the evening he continued his erotic play on her senses. At midnight they sat at the table holding hands, talking.

He pulled her onto his lap. "Happy New Year, Darlin', may the beginning of this New Year be the beginning of our lives." He said then kissed her.

# CHAPTER TEN

When they were leaving the club Kyle grabbed the unopened bottle of champagne. While they were undressing for bed Kayla woke up. Abby dressed again, going to nurse her. She met Roberta in the hallway.

"I'll get her, you go back to bed." Abby told her.

Roberta nodded and went back to her room. Abby went to the nursery and locked the door. Picking up her daughter, she attempted to nurse, giving up as Kayla became louder. Kyle went to the nursery when he heard his daughter. He found the door locked.

"Abby, what's wrong? Why is the door locked?" He asked.

"Go to bed, Kyle." She said.

"Open the door." He demanded, pounding on it.

"Stop, Kyle. You're going to wake everyone up." She said.

Kerry began to whimper. She went to his cradle. "Great! What else can happen?"

"Kyle, what's going on?" Judy asked, coming down the hall.

"Abby's in the nursery with the door locked." He told her.

Judy knocked on the door. "Abby, open the door." She said.

Abby went to the door, unlocked it, opened it and motioned her mother in. Kyle stepped through the door. Judy went back to bed.

"Why did you lock the door?" Kyle asked.

"I wanted to be alone." Abby answered.

"In the nursery? Surely you could have thought of a better way to tell me you've changed your mind." He snapped.

"Changed my mind?" She said puzzled.

"Yes. While we were at the club you were safe enough. Here, there isn't anything to stop me from making love to you. You're locking me out again."

"I wasn't locking you out."

Kyle took his screaming daughter from Abby, gently bouncing her in his arms.

"Tend to Kerry." He said gruffly.

Confused at the change of subject, Abby obediently went to her son. She settled in the rocker to nurse him.

"You aren't a very good liar, Querida."

Startled, she looked at him. "What?"

"You're locking me out because you're afraid of the feelings you've been having this evening."

"That's absurd."

"Is it? In our bedroom, not twenty-four hours ago, I could have made love to you. My mistake was remembering too soon Dr. Cooper's orders of abstinence for six weeks."

"No, your mistake is in thinking I'm unable to resist you."

"Shall we try out my theory?"

Abby was spared answering when Kayla let out a burp on her father's shoulder. She began to laugh.

"What's so funny? Kayla spit up on me and you're laughing."

"She has gas." Abby announced unnecessarily.

"It isn't funny, Abby. Now I have to shower and change."

Abby giggled. "Welcome to the wonderful world of fatherhood."

At his look of menace, she brought her laughter under control. "Give her to me and go clean up."

Kyle handed his daughter to Abby, and went to shower and change. Meanwhile, Abby tended her children. She finished nursing Kerry, changed him then settled him back in his cradle. She nursed and changed Kayla. She was settling her back into her cradle when Kyle came back to the nursery.

"Was there something you wanted?" She asked, looking into his eyes to avoid looking at his naked torso.

"Come to bed, Querida." He commanded.

Abby swallowed hard. "I'll just tidy up here, then I'll come to bed." She told him.

"Think again, Sweetheart. You are my wife, you will come to bed now. Remember, our bargain also includes sleeping in my bed."

"If I refuse?"

"I don't think you will. I have very effective ways of persuading you to change your mind." He walked toward her. She backed away from him until her back came up against the wall.

"You wouldn't force me... Dr. Cooper said..."

"No, Sweetheart, I won't force myself on you. I won't have to. You'll be a very willing partner in your own seduction. Before I'm through you'll be begging for release. There are more ways to make love than the conventional."

Bending over her and placing a hand on either side of her head, he kissed her. When he drew away she was trembling in need of his possession. Before she could gather her wits he picked her up, carrying her to their bed. He laid her in the middle of the bed following her down. Kissing her again he slowly removed her clothes. Letting his mouth wander over the expanse of skin he'd exposed, he quickly discarded his own clothing.

"Touch me, Querida. I want to feel your hands on me." He ordered his voice filled with desire.

Abby ran her hands over his chest. Holding onto his shoulders, she rained kisses over his face and chest. She nipped at his lower lip, his upper lip, and one hardened male nipple, then the other. Kyle pushed her back against the pillows, holding her hands above her head. He suckled each breast.

"Kyle, help me. I'm burning up."

"Relax, Love. I'm going to make love to you slow and easy."

He showed her how to make love to him with her hands, mouth and body without completing their union.

"Show me you want me, Darlin.' Tell me you need me. Just as I want and need you." He ordered gruffly.

"No, Kyle." He stiffened. "You aren't alone. I want and need you as you want and need me." She told him. Adding to herself, *"but wanting and needing aren't love."*

She kissed and touched him as she had longed to since the first time he had made love to her. She coaxed a response from him and demanded he assuage her hunger. He slipped his fingers down the silky length of her thigh. She arched and bucked at the promise he gave when he slipped his fingers inside her. It wasn't her first time, but his love play made her believe it was. She demanded release from the fiery prison he'd taken her to. Though they're bodies weren't joined, Abby's release was like nothing she'd ever experienced. She clung to him as wave after wave of pleasure coursed through her. He guided her hands to his arousal. Holding him in her hands, she cupped and stroked him, feeling his life force pulse through him and spill over. Kyle's release brought stronger, renewed waves of pleasure to her. Sated, Abby cried tears of happiness.

"Darlin'?" He asked tensely.

"I didn't know...I never imagined..." She said happily. He silenced her with a kiss.

"Sleep Sweetheart."

Rolling on top of him, she said, "Sleep? I'm much too wide awake to sleep."

She used her hands to tease him. When she found the evidence he wasn't sleepy either, she laughed. "You don't really want me to go to sleep, do you?" She teased, rubbing against him provocatively. He rolled her over, trapping her beneath him.

"You're insatiable woman."

Doctor's orders prevented them from joining, but this time their loving was wild and abandoned. She soared with the eagles and landed with the grace of a swan. When he urged her to sleep, she teased him by casting aspersions on his manhood. Growling, he forced her onto her back. When she laughed he took her over and over, proving his manhood until she lay limp and sated in his arms. This time when he suggested she sleep, she did, quite contentedly.

When Abby awoke she was laying on her side. Kyle held her spoon fashion, his arm draped over her, one hand cradling a swollen, aching breast. If she moved, she'd wake him up. Not wanting to wake him, she lay against him as dreams began to play in her mind. She closed her eyes. If only Kyle loved her, their marriage would be as loving as last night had been. She dreamt of the life they would have, laying still as the scenes played themselves out. As she dreamt, Kyle awoke to find Abby smiling. He kissed her. Thinking it was her dream she kissed him back. Kyle bent his head to capture one rosy bud in his mouth it sprang to life. Abby arched into his mouth seeking the pleasure he promised. What a wonderful dream. She put her arms around his neck to urge his warm mouth to her waiting lips. He captured her mouth with his. Sliding his tongue inside, he brought her to full arousal. Suddenly the dream was brought crashing down. Reality set in when Kayla and Kerry demanded to be fed.

Abby's eyes flew open, meeting Kyle's hungry blue gaze. Her expression showed surprise at finding her husband making love to her. His eyes, filled with passion a moment ago, became shuttered and unreadable.

"I wasn't dreaming?" She stated.

"No. Disappointed?" He said.

"Yes and no."

He arched a brow at her.

"No, I was enjoying our morning lovemaking. Yes, I have to get up to feed our children." She said.

"You could always come back to bed and we could finish what we started." He suggested.

"We have guests, remember."

He rolled onto his back, allowing her to sit up. His shirt lay at the foot of the bed. She pulled it to her and put it on. When she stood the shirt fell below her knees. She went to nurse her hungry children. Once in the nursery, she shut the door. She went to her children, assuring them that she was there and they would soon have their breakfast.

While tending to them, she remembered Kyle's lovemaking. He hadn't said he loved her. If all she was allowed were the one-year he'd stipulated, she'd accept knowing she loved him.

Kyle showered and dressed after Abby left their bed. He went to the kitchen. Pouring himself coffee, he was surprised to find Quinton sitting at the dining room table.

He had expected his mother or Judy.

"Good morning. What has you up so early this morning?" He asked, sitting across from Quinton.

Quinton laughed harshly. "My blonde, green-eyed neighbor. I figured if I left before she came out, things would defrost around here." He admitted candidly.

"Running away, little brother?" Kyle said.

"Strategic retreat. Regrouping my forces." Quinton corrected.

Kyle laughed. "Strategic retreat? Pointless and futile, all out warfare would be more to your advantage."

"I'll take my chances with silent attack. It is effective and she won't know what hit her."

Abby went to her room to shower and dress. When she gathered up the courage, she went to face Kyle. Entering the kitchen soundlessly, she poured herself coffee, adding milk. Going into the dining room just as soundlessly, she turned to leave as the tension crackled between Kyle and Quinton. Kyle's words stopped her. "Come in, Sweetheart. Don't let us stop you from enjoying your morning ritual."

"You know Kyle, you really have to stop doing that, it's beginning to get eerie. I'm not intruding?" Abby said.

"Yes, but it's a welcome intrusion." Quinton told her.

Abby sat in the chair next to Kyle. He leaned over, brushing the backs of his fingers against her cheek. "Good morning, again." He said smiling.

"Good morning." She said turning her head to brush her lips across his knuckles.

He drew his breath in sharply. Putting his hands in her hair, he drew her to him for his kiss. They drew apart for air. Abby looked in Quinton's direction, blinking in surprise.

"He left, Love. While we were otherwise engaged, Quint thought it best to make his exit." Kyle told her.

"Is he all right?" She asked.

"Quint is always all right. He's just had the wind knocked out of him. He'll be back to his old self in no time." He said.

Abby didn't get the chance to answer because their families began to wander in. The morning was spent helping Abby's family get ready for their flight back to Shelby. Kyle's parents gathered their belongings to put them in the car for their return home.

"You'll bring my girl home to visit." Andrew ordered Kyle as he got into the car.

"Just as soon as I can. It may be a while, I have months of work backlogged." Kyle answered.

"But you'll call?" Judy asked Abby.

"Yes, Mama, every week." Abby promised, hugging her.

"Don't worry about Abby. We'll check in on her." Roberta assured them.

That evening the house was quiet after everyone had gone. Kerry and Kayla were settled for the night and Agnes wasn't due back for another week. Kyle and Abby sat in the living room drinking coffee in front of the roaring fireplace. She sat her coffee cup on the table next to her chair. Laying her head back, she sighed.

"Something wrong?" He asked.

"No, just tired, it's been a long week." She answered.

"Did you enjoy it?" He asked.

"Oh yes, thank you again. Having our families together for Christmas was wonderful. Do you think we could do it again next Christmas?" She asked excitedly.

"If you like. I don't want your gratitude, Abby."

He told her with his eyes what he did want. Unsure she was able to give him what he asked, she looked away from him.

"You can't wish it away, Abby." At her silence he went on. "Last night we made love as we did the night we met."

"We can't turn back time, Kyle."

"No, but we can change the course of the future. Starting now, this moment, we'll have a normal marriage until one or the other of us decides to dissolve it."

"We agreed we'd dissolve it after one year."

"I've changed my mind."

Abby had accepted the one-year knowing it would hurt when the separation came. Prolonging the marriage would only make the pain unbearable.

"You can't do that!"

Ignoring her protest, he said, "We'll take each day as it comes. If we divorce you'll have everything you and the children need."

"*I'll have everything I need except you.*" She told him silently.

Kyle knew Abby loved him. Her outright refusal to tell him sent him into action. He knew two people who could help him make Abby believe in love and trust again. Millie and Andrew. He called on them for help. "Fill the house with children. Tabi loves children and won't be able to resist loving and nurturing them. Some of it is bound to spill over onto you." Andrew told him.

"Dr. Cooper advised her not to get pregnant again for at least another year." Kyle said.

"Never let her think you aren't there even when you aren't. Make her aware of your presence in her life." Andrew said.

Kyle realized Andrew knew Abby better than he did. He took advantage of that knowledge.

"You mean manipulate her into admitting she doesn't want to live without me?" Kyle asked.

"No, manipulating Tabi will only make her resent you. Be subtle in reminding her what she'll be missing if she lets you leave her life. Show her your love." Andrew suggested.

Kyle read between the lines.

Making love to her! He knew she couldn't resist his seduction no matter how much she wanted to pretend otherwise. He'd use her sensual awareness of him to seduce her, and then he'd have her where he wanted her, in his arms, by his side, where she belonged.

"Thanks, Andrew. I have to go."

Kyle hung up on Andrew's laughter at his determination to get to Tabi. He thought back to the conversation he'd had with Quint on New Year's morning. He'd told Quinton that all out warfare would be more to his advantage in dealing with Andrea. Quinton had been right when he'd said he was planning a strategic retreat to regroup his forces.

Kyle called Millie to ask for her help in planning Abby's seduction. Millie agreed to help in any way she could. He only need let her know what he wanted done. When Abby arose in the mornings Kyle was already gone, but he left little reminders of himself around the house to remind her of his shameless sensuality, and that he wanted her. Over the following weeks Kyle planned the destruction of her final barrier, overcoming her fear of loving him. He seduced without completion.

As the weeks went by Kyle counted them until Abby would be his wife in every sense of the word. He became more and more frustrated at the forced abstinence. Abby was feeling the frustration too. She wished Kyle would make love to her or stop the sensual seduction. But did she really want him to stop? No! Valentine's Day morning Agnes came into their room with a breakfast tray. She sat it on Abby's lap and left. On the tray was not her breakfast, but one of Kyle's handkerchiefs and a note. Picking up the handkerchief, she wondered what it meant. Kyle's scent was on it. She inhaled deeply the scent that was so uniquely Kyle and read the note.

*Agnes has been given strict orders that you're not to be disturbed today; she's taking the children out for the day. Take the day to pamper yourself.*
                              *Love, Kyle*

Abby stretched and smiled. She would take a nice, long hot bubble bath. Getting out of bed, she went into the bathroom to run her bath.

Pulling back the shower curtain, she gave a delighted laugh. In the bathtub sat a giant panda. There was a note attached to his chest.

*Happy Valentine's Day Darlin', we have a date this evening. Wear something special.*

*Love, Kyle*

Abby took the toy out of the tub and put him on the bed. She ran her bath adding bubble bath. Taking a leisurely bath, she relaxed and soaked until she was as wrinkled as a prune. After her bath she dressed and went downstairs. Going into the kitchen she poured a cup of coffee adding milk. Sitting next to the coffee maker was another note held up by a small box.

*Wear these this evening to accompany your necklace and ring.*

*Love, Kyle*

In the box were opal earrings to match the necklace and ring Kyle had given her.

"What are you planning, Kyle?" She wondered aloud, tears forming in her eyes.

Abby took her coffee into the living room. As she sat down the phone rang.

She answered, "Masterson's."

"Hello, Tabitha, this is Aunt Millie." Millie greeted.

"Hi, Aunt Millie, how are you?" Abby said.

"Bored, I'm calling to invite you to lunch and to go shopping." Millie told her.

"I was going to do some shopping today. What time?" Abby asked.

"How about noon, pick me up at my house."

"All right." Abby checked her watch. "I'll be there in half an hour."

As Abby drove to Millie's she thought about what she would wear for her date with Kyle. Millie stood outside waiting for Abby. She walked to the car when Abby pulled into the drive.

"What shall we do first, lunch or shop?" Millie asked.

"Shop, we can work up an appetite." Abby said.

She told Millie about her date with Kyle. Millie knew just where they should get the something special. After lunch they did more shopping, then Abby took Millie home. When she pulled into the driveway Kyle's Corvette sat in the drive. She wondered why he was home early. She checked her watch. Her eyes widened. He wasn't early she was late. She hurried into the house with her packages.

"I'm sorry I'm late. I was shopping and..."

She stopped. Kyle was leaning on the fireplace with two glasses of champagne in his hands.

"Good evening, Darlin'. How was your day?" He drawled.

Abby stared at him. He was dressed in a black tuxedo that hugged his body like a second skin. She dropped the packages unnoticed to the floor. Kyle walked toward her, handing her a glass of champagne when he reached her. She took it with a trembling hand. He kissed her. When the kiss ended she took a long drink of her champagne.

"I probably should get dressed." She suggested in an unsteady voice.

"That's a very good idea.  Use one of the spare bedrooms down the hall." He told her.

Abby nodded and went to get dressed. When she finished she went in search of Kyle.  He wasn't in the living room where she'd left him, but there was another note.

*"My lady, I await your arrival in our chamber."*
*My Love,*

*Your Faithful Knight*

She went up the stairs to their room.  She was pleasantly surprised to find a table set for two in front of the fireplace.  It was glowing and the only other light in the room came from the candles on the table.

"It's beautiful, Kyle." She told him.

"Not as beautiful as you."  He declared in a husky whisper next to her ear.

Abby turned slightly to look at him.  His mouth grazed her cheek.  He was watching her intently.  She was stunning in a strapless white gown.  It molded her breasts down to her hips where it flared out and fell below her knees.  She had applied a light dusting of cosmetics to enhance her features.  At her throat and on her ears she wore the opals Kyle had given her. She'd left her hair loose to hang down her back.

Neither could tear their gaze away.  Kyle gently touched his lips to hers. At her warm response, he deepened the kiss. He pulled her closer to let her feel his arousal. She gasped, squirming closer for better contact. While he kissed her all thought left her mind. Abby allowed the sensations he was bringing to life run over her. There were no doctor's orders to bar them from a complete union. Demanding her own rights, she used her hands to touch and tease. Exploring the contours of his chest, she tore at the buttons of his shirt. He groaned, when she became the temptress and he the tempted. Abby took over the role of seductress. She urged him toward the bed, pushing against him as she kissed his chest. She trailed hot kisses along his throat when he moved back as she wanted him to.

When his legs came into contact with the bed she shoved him back, falling on top of him. His hands came up to mold her to him. Slowly she undressed him, not losing contact with his body. No words were needed to express their love.

He tugged at the zipper of her dress. It gave way to let him pull the dress over her curves. To his surprise she was wearing a white bustier with matching thong and a garter belt. It took him over the edge. Stripping her of her clothes, he fumbled in his nightstand for a foil packet and sheathed himself. Thrusting quick and deep he brought their union to completion. They made love for hours, falling asleep in each other's arms.

Abby awoke when Kayla and Kerry began crying. Kyle assured her Agnes was with them.

"You know this wasn't supposed to happen." He told her, indicating their still clinging bodies.

Abby drew the sheet around her, backing away from him.

"No, Abby you won't pull away from me again. I hadn't intended to seduce you until after we'd eaten." He said.

She blushed pink.

He laughed. "Are you hungry?" He asked.

"A little." She answered.

"Let's see what we can salvage from supper." He said taking her hand to help her out of bed.

She drew away from him again.

"I told you not to pull away from me again!" He growled.

She lowered her eyes. Just above a whisper, she said, "I haven't got anything to put on."

"You haven't got anything ... good Lord woman, we've spent the better part of the evening making love and you're worried about getting out of bed nude." He grumbled.

Abby pulled the sheet higher above her breasts. "I am not getting out of this bed until I have something to put on." She stated firmly.

"You're serious?"

"Quite."

He climbed out of bed. Grabbing his briefs and pants he put them on. "Of all the ridiculous things I have ever heard in my life."

Kyle gathered his shirt from the floor where Abby had thrown it. Walking to her, he handed it to her.

"This should cover you properly enough."

She took the shirt. Putting it on, she climbed out of bed. "Thank you."

"Are you through, or must I tolerate watching you hide yourself from me?" Kyle asked angrily.

"I'm not hiding. My body has gone through some changes since I became pregnant." She told him honestly.

"All this nonsense over changes in your body?" He asked annoyed. Abby scooted across the bed when he came toward her.

"Let me see."

"No."

"I want to see, Abby. Come here."

Reluctantly she went to him. When she was within reach, he pulled her toward him lifting the shirt. She closed her eyes to avoid the repulsion in his eyes at the changes her pregnancy had made.

"These were made by our children. How could they be anything but beautiful?" He said bending to kiss her abdomen.

Abby gasped and tensed as he kissed the only physical evidence left from her pregnancy.

"Relax, Abby, let me love you." He told her.

He used his mouth and hands to love her. He lingered just above her womanhood until he felt her relax. Lowering his mouth, he pushed his tongue into her core of desire. Lowering her gently to the bed, he loved her with his mouth and hands the way he had with his body. Abby cried his name over and over as her body responded to his lovemaking. Soon afterward she was asleep again. Kyle moved her to the top of the bed pulling the blankets over her. He went to the table to see what could be salvaged from supper.

While he sat eating he watched Abby sleep. She slept peacefully, reaching for him once. Not finding him, she moved to his pillow.

Inhaling his scent, she smiled. Hugging it closer, she drifted back to sleep. Her hair was spread across her pillow, her dark lashes lay against her flushed cheeks and one cheek lay cupped in her hand. In an unusual pang of self-doubt, Kyle wondered if he'd made a mistake forcing her to marry him. Would it be another mistake to continue the marriage after their first anniversary? Probably, but he didn't have much choice. He'd love her for the rest of his life and couldn't imagine living without her. Frustrated by his inner musings, he stood up and paced the length of the bedroom. This was getting him nowhere. He went to get a drink, continuing his pacing in the study as he nursed the glass of Scotch. He violently cursed himself for his stupidity in the forced marriage.

Kyle was gone when Abby awoke. She found him in the study, striding briskly back and forth across the room.

"Kyle?" She questioned.

Startled, he looked up. She was beautiful. After their night of lovemaking she was even more so, especially wearing his shirt. He smiled. Maybe that was the answer. He'd keep her dressed in his shirts; Lord only knew what the sight did to his libido.

"Did you sleep well?" He asked.

"Yes, thanks, what time is it?" She asked.

He looked at the watch on his wrist. "About two a.m. How are you feeling?"

She blushed. He chuckled.

Abby put her hands on her hips. "Just what is so funny?"

Kyle put down his Scotch and walked to her. Pushing her hands aside, he replaced them with his, pulling her close. The mixture of their earlier lovemaking and her scent was heady.

"You are, Darlin'."

"Kyle Masterson don't you dare laugh at me. I'll have you know because of your supper, or lack of, I have sore muscles I didn't know I had."

He laughed outright then. She became indignant.

He brought himself under control. "A warm bath should help relieve your...should soothe your... damn, go take a warm bath, Tabitha."

Surprised at his use of her given name, Abby stared at him. She temporarily forgot the aches caused by his lovemaking.

"What's wrong?"

"You called me Tabitha."

"It is your name."

"Yes, but you've never called me Tabitha."

"You object."

"No."

"Good, let's get you into that bath. If you're very good, I may join you."

He raised his eyebrows lasciviously urging her up the stairs for her bath. While she ran her bath, he went into the bedroom to clear away supper. After finishing he went to check on Abby. He had very definite ideas on how to take a bath, none of which included bathing. He opened the drawer in the nightstand next to his side of the bed. And withdrew a few foil packets, stuffing them into his pockets.

"I told you to take a bath not fall asleep." He teased.

She sat up. "I must have dozed off. I'll be out in twenty minutes." She said slipping back into the water.

"To prevent you from drowning yourself, I'll join you." He said.

"Come in, the water's fine." She invited.

Removing his pants and briefs, he climbed in, yelping at the water's temperature.

"I said warm, not scalding."

He settled into the water. Taking the pouf, he poured bath gel on it. Leaning over, Kyle ran it slowly, seductively over her. He continued his gentle ministrations luring her closer until she lay atop him. Draining the tub he fumbled in his pants pocket, pulling out one of the packets.

Sheathing himself, he thrust inside her, surprising her. "Kyle!"

It was the last coherent thing she was able to say for quite some time. Kyle was sitting in a chair by the fireplace drinking coffee when Abby awoke.

"Good morning, Sweetheart. How did you sleep?" He asked when he heard her moving around in their bed.

"Was I asleep? I thought I was awake at two o'clock this morning." She teased.

"You were wide-awake, Darlin" He assured her.

She looked at the bedside clock. It was past noon.

"Kayla and Kerry are going to start thinking we've abandoned them." Oblivious of her nudity, she climbed out of bed to go into the bathroom for a shower.

"I'm through with the shower if you want it." She said, coming back into the room wearing his robe.

Kyle went to take a shower. Abby was dressed when he came out of the shower. Kyle dressed. She straightened the room. She removed the sheets and other bedclothes, putting them into a bundle recalling the previous night's activities.

"Kyle?" She said.

"Yes, Love." He answered.

"We didn't... I didn't think... Kyle what if I get pregnant again?" She asked alarmed.

"Would that be so awful?" He asked holding his breath.

"Yes. No. You know what Dr. Cooper said about getting pregnant too soon."

"Don't you want more children?" He asked aloud. *"Or don't you want more of my children?"* He added silently.

"Of course I want more children. I'd love lots of children, but I'd rather we had some time with the ones we already have."

"Don't worry, Darlin', I took care of protecting you against pregnancy. I wouldn't go against doctor's orders."

He'd give her as many children as she wanted if it meant having her with him for the next, oh say... fifty years. He thought to himself smiling. Abby put fresh linens on the bed. They went down to brunch.

"Good afternoon, Mr. and Mrs. Masterson." Agnes greeted them.

"Good afternoon, Agnes." Abby and Kyle greeted in unison. "How were our babies last night?" Abby asked.

"They were little angels." Agnes told her.

Abby went to talk to Kerry and Kayla.  "Good afternoon, angels. How are you?"

Kyle joined her in greeting their children. "Good afternoon, Precious."

"Good afternoon, Champ." He said, laying a hand along each of their cheeks.

Kayla and Kerry responded to his touch and voice, smiling and turning their blue eyes on him.

"They know I'm talking to them." Kyle said awed. "Of course they do." Abby said.

Kyle and Abby spent a little more time talking to their children then went to the table for brunch. Agnes served them, and then went back to the kitchen.  Having just realized that Kyle should be at work, Abby blurted, "You aren't supposed to be here."

"I beg your pardon.  Last time I checked this was still my home." He stated.

"That's not what I meant. Don't you have to go to work?" She asked. "I took the day off." He told her.

"Oh."

"You sound disappointed."

"No, I didn't want you to think you had to stay home because we...so I'd... I wouldn't want you to neglect your business."

"We won't go bankrupt because I took the day off."

"I didn't mean that!"

"I know.  Relax, Sweetheart, it was a joke."

She looked at him, searching his eyes for humor. She found it in the bright blue depths.

"If making love to you means losing the business, I'd rather lose the business than stop making love to you." He told her honestly.

Abby blushed. He pulled her close, kissing her. Kerry and Kayla let them know they'd had enough of being neglected by their parents.

"I'm sorry to interrupt, Mrs. Masterson, but the little ones are hungry and refuse to take the bottle." Agnes said from the doorway.

"Please bring them in." Abby said beginning to unbutton her shirt.

She remembered Kyle's annoyance when she'd prepared to nurse in the living room Christmas Day. She buttoned her shirt again.

"Weren't you going to nurse?" He asked puzzled.

"Yes, but I remember how annoyed you were when I started to nurse in the living room Christmas Day." She replied.

"I really don't mind, if it's comfortable for you." He told her.

"I'll go upstairs." She said.

Annoyed, he said, "I've told you I don't mind. It is a natural part of motherhood."

"You're sure you don't mind?"

"Damn it Abby, I've just said that I don't."

Agnes brought Kayla and Kerry into the dining room, then went back to clean up the kitchen.

# CHAPTER ELEVEN

While Abby nursed Kayla and Kerry the phone rang. After answering it, Agnes came into the dining room saying, "It's for you, Mrs. Masterson. It's Roberta Masterson." Abby started to get up. Kyle gently pushed her back into her chair. "I'll take it, you have your hands full." He told her.

He walked into the kitchen to answer the phone. "Hello, Mother."

"Kyle? I asked to speak to Tabitha. Where is she? She hasn't left you has she?" Roberta asked.

"No, Mother. Abby can't come to the phone, she has her hands full." Kyle told her.

"Tell her to come to the phone. I want to speak to her." Roberta demanded.

"I'll have her call you back. She's nursing Kayla and Kerry." Kyle said.

"Oh, well, then there's no rush. I've promised her something and wanted to give it to her today. Have her call me at her convenience." Roberta hung up.

Kyle went back into the dining room. He was both amused and bewildered.

"What did your mother want?" Abby asked, concerned by the emotions chasing across his face.

"She wants you to call her back at your convenience. She said she promised you something and wanted to give it to you today." Kyle told her.

Abby searched her memory for something Roberta had promised her.

She blushed a bright pink when she remembered.

"Is there something you want to share with me? Something I should know before you call mother?" Kyle asked.

"What?  No, I'll call her after I've settled the children down for their nap." Abby said.

"You're sure you don't want to talk about it."

The color that had begun to leave Abby's face, now came back full of life.

"Mind your own business, Kyle.  Some things a woman shares with her mother-in-law are secret and should remain so."

"I'd give almost anything to know what mother promised you to make you blush that way."  Kyle murmured huskily.

Abby ignored his comment and used all her powers of concentration to come up with something else to think about. After she finished nursing, Kyle helped her take their children upstairs to the nursery. They gave them their baths, dressed them and settled them down for a nap. Abby went into the study to return Roberta's call.

"Hi, Mama, it's Abby.  Kyle said you wanted me to return your call." She said when Roberta answered the phone.

"Are you free to go shopping today?" Roberta asked.

"Kyle took the day off.  If he hasn't made special plans I'll call you back. We can set up a time and place to meet." Abby agreed.

"Don't put your plans on hold for me.  We can have lunch and go shopping another time." Roberta said.

"I'm sure Kyle won't mind. I'll call you back."

"I'll expect your call."

"All right, bye Mama."

Abby hung up the phone. She went in search of Kyle. Finding him in the living room, she went in to talk to him.

"Did you call mother?" He asked when she sat down.

"Mm hm. Do you have special plans for today?" Abby asked.

"No, why?" He asked.

"Your mother wants me to have lunch and go shopping with her." She told him.

"The royal summons. I wonder what she's up to. What did mother promise you, Querida? It has to be something pretty special for her to interfere."

"What makes you think she's up to something? Why do you think she's interfering? She may want to get better acquainted with me. It isn't unusual for a mother to want to get to know her son's wife."

"Mother has always made it a point not to interfere in the choices Quinton and I have made. Including having any kind of relationship with the women we've been involved with. She waits for them to come to her. She's up to something. The question is, what?"

An hour later Abby was informed why her mother-in-law had invited her to go shopping and have lunch.

"First, I don't usually stick my nose into my sons' private lives. Second, I had no idea Kyle was so like his father. For that, I must apologize." Roberta began.

"An apology isn't necessary. Kyle is a grown man; he does exactly as he pleases. A bulldozer wouldn't stand a chance against him." Abby told her.

"Unfortunately, you are right. Which brings me back to why I invited you to join me today. Remember I promised to tell you the story of my courtship with Kyle's father." Roberta said.

Abby nodded. When she opened her mouth to forestall the story, Roberta put up her hand.

"When I met Kin I was engaged to his brother. I was the direct opposite of what Harry preferred in a woman. He isn't like the rest of the Masterson men. I was exuberant, bold, and impetuous. A shrew, with a tart, barbed tongue on the surface."

A waiter came to the table to take their order. "What can I get for you ladies?" He asked.

"Give us a few more minutes." Roberta said.

"Yes, ma'am." He said and went back to his duties.

"I'm sorry, where was I?" Roberta asked.

"When you met Kyle's father." Abby prompted.

"Yes, I did things for myself, never caring if I hurt anyone in the process. I intended to marry Harry no matter what anyone said or did. I didn't love him as he should have been loved. Kin saw through me the first time we met."

Roberta motioned for the waiter to take their order. He seemed to appear from nowhere.

"I'll have the turkey club and iced tea." Roberta told him.

"And you, ma'am?" He said turning to Abby. "I'll have the same and a side salad." Abby said.

"Enjoy your meal." He told them, and left.

"Kin told me he wasn't about to stand by and watch his brother marry the woman who belonged to him."

Abby gasped at the audacity and shook her head. Roberta laughed. "Yes. I asked him how he dared speak to me in such a manner. I proceeded to walk away from him. He grabbed my hand, turned me to him and kissed me."

Abby's mouth dropped open. Belatedly, she closed it. "Please don't tell me anymore." She pleaded.

Silently she wished the waiter would appear from nowhere again. Her wish went unfulfilled.

"I haven't come to the interesting part yet." Roberta said.

"I really don't think this is any of my business." Abby said.

"How else will you learn to deal with my arrogant son?" Roberta asked.

"I...perhaps...in time...I really have no idea." Abby admitted.

"No, nor will you. He already has a head start. If you don't catch up soon, you never will."

The waiter brought their food. Abby dug into hers ravenously. She hadn't eaten much of the brunch Agnes had served earlier that day. Roberta smiled. There would be only one reason her daughter-in-law would eat so heartily. It wasn't because Kyle starved her. Abby saw Roberta's smile. She looked at her plate. "I'm sorry. I seem to be rather hungry today." She said after she finished chewing.

"It's all right, child. That's another thing Masterson men have in common." Roberta told her.

Abby looked puzzled.

"Increasing a woman's appetite." Roberta said smiling.

Abby was drinking her iced tea and began choking. The waiter appeared and clapped her gently on the back.

"Are you all right, Mrs. Masterson? Is there anything I can get you?" He asked.

"A hole to crawl into." Abby begged silently.

"Yes, I'm fine. No, nothing thanks." She said aloud.

She thanked him for his concern and assured him again that she was fine.

He went back to his work.

"How did he know my name?" Abby asked.

"I told the manager you're my daughter-in-law when we came in." Roberta told her.

"How?" Abby said.

"You were looking at the décor. It is lovely isn't it?" Roberta said.

Abby looked around at the colors on the walls, carpet and tables. She hadn't really seen it when they came in. She'd been too nervous about this meeting with Roberta. The restaurant was decorated in coral and ivory.

"Kyle doesn't own this restaurant, does he?" Abby asked.

"No, why do you ask?" Roberta said.

"Our home is decorated with these same colors." Abby reminded her.

"This is his favorite restaurant. He started coming here about the same time he met you. When we'd meet for lunch, he'd tell me it reminded him of someone. He'd never tell me who. Now I know it was you."

Abby thought Kyle had lied when he'd told his mother he'd redecorated the house for her. The restaurant reminded him of her. She hadn't told Kyle her favorite colors on the night they'd met. She sat back in her chair. She gazed thoughtfully about the room. Her heart gave a joyous leap. Maybe he did love her after all. Roberta hated to bring Abby out of her inner musings, especially if they involved Kyle. But she didn't have a choice.

"Tabitha, people are beginning to stare and the manager is getting nervous." Roberta told her.

"What?" Abby asked.

"The other patrons are beginning to think you haven't recovered from your choking spell." Roberta said.

Abby looked around her. Seeing the anxious faces, she smiled to reassure them she was fine.

"I was thinking." Abby said.

"About what?" Roberta asked.

"Oh, nothing really." Abby told her, waving it off.

"If you'd rather not share it with me." Roberta said.

"It's not that. Do you believe in psychic connections?"

"I'm not sure I understand what you mean."

"Nothing, I'm being foolish. Before long you'll think your son married a fruitcake."

"Nonsense. Please explain what you meant."

Abby shook her head. At Roberta's look of consternation, she tried to explain.

"Except for a few times, I've always known when Kyle is nearby. I feel his presence before I actually see him. He knows what I'm going to do almost before I do. And you just said this restaurant reminded him of me."

Roberta's eyes widened. "I don't understand. Perhaps you told him your favorite colors."

Abby shook her head. "No. We did a lot of talking the night we met, but nothing that personal."

"You were meant for each other. You have a bond that goes beyond the senses."

"Not ESP? Kyle and Andie asked me if I thought it was ESP."

"What do you think?"

"I think it's an eerie sort of coincidence and it's very annoying."

"Whatever it is, it has brought you and my son together. Don't question it, accept that it has brought you together as one and build your lives on it."

Abby and Roberta finished lunch then went shopping.

"You'll need to refurbish your wardrobe after having the babies."

"That's not necessary. I have all of my old clothes."

"They aren't going to fit as they once did. You'll lose the weight, but your proportions are different." Roberta told her.

"I have tried to wear some of my larger clothes, they are a little snug in places." Abby admitted.

"I remember when I tried on my clothes after I miscarried my first pregnancy. I was determined to prove I was still attractive."

"You miscarried your first pregnancy. Kyle didn't..."

"We didn't tell Kyle or Quinton. It was a very difficult time in our lives. When I became pregnant with Kyle I kept the news from his father."

"If this is bringing back unpleasant memories..."

"No. When Kin learned I was pregnant with our first child, he was ecstatic. He insisted we marry. On our wedding day I began having pains. He took me to the hospital."

Roberta looked through the clothes on the racks. Abby barely detected her shaking hands. She hugged Roberta, sharing the remembered pain.

"When the doctor told us I was losing the baby, I ordered Kin out of my life. No amount of reasoning was going to change my mind."

"I'm sorry, Mama. But you and Papa are married and have two wonderful sons." Abby stated.

"Yes, but with a great deal of difficulty. I saw my miscarriage as a failure to Kin as well as myself. Kin still insisted we be married. I refused, believing he only wanted to marry me to salvage his pride."

Abby shook her head, not believing her father-in-law could be so cruel.

"Of course my reasoning was wrong, but I wasn't going to admit it. How could Kin want to marry me when I'd lost his beloved daughter?" Abby followed Roberta through the store as she chose clothes to restore her wardrobe. Roberta picked out pastels and lighter colors that would highlight Abby's creamy complexion.

"Papa must have loved you very much, otherwise why would he insist you marry him after the miscarriage?" Abby said.

"I didn't believe he loved me. In fact, I told him to find a woman who loved him. And of course I thought that would make him believe I wasn't in love with him." Roberta told her.

"But you were in love with him, you must have been." Abby insisted.

"Of course I was, child. Why else would I have tried to push him into another woman's arms? Guilt helps a woman make some pretty foolish mistakes. You always hurt the ones you love." Roberta stated.

"You became pregnant with Kyle. How? What?"

Roberta looked into their shopping cart. She led Abby to the checkout. After paying for their purchases, Roberta took Abby to a small coffee shop. They gave their order to the waitress who appeared.

"Kin was very persistent. On the first anniversary of my miscarriage I agreed to meet him for dinner. I conceived Kyle that night. I was lonely, scared and miserable. I didn't think one night of passion could change my life so drastically."

"You didn't tell Papa you were pregnant."

"No, I avoided him as I had after the miscarriage. Kin took the bull by the horns, as the saying goes, and took matters into his own hands. To this day I don't know how, but he learned I was pregnant again. Before I knew what was happening, he'd gotten me to agree to marry him and admit I was as in love him as he was with me.  And the rest is history." She said tearfully.

Abby wiped the tears from her own cheeks. "Oh, Mama, what a beautiful story.  Anyone who sees you together can see the love you share." She said tearfully.

"As well as everyone can see the love between you and my stubborn son.  When Kyle was born Kindred wrote a poem for me.  I always carry it with me." Roberta said, opening her purse.

She handed the paper to Abby.  She took it, reading the poem.

## IF LOVE WERE WISHES

If Love were wishes, and wishes could come true, you'd have no more wishing to do.

If Love was dreams, and dreams could come true, you'd have no more dreaming to do.

If Love was hope, and hope always could come true, you'd have no more hoping to do.

If Love were happiness, I would wish it, dream it and hope it for you, because it is with love I give them to you.

Abby started to hand the paper back to Roberta, wiping away more tears. Roberta took Abby's hand in her own.  "Please keep it. I have it here." She said placing her hand over her heart. "It's time to pass it on to my daughter."

"Thank you, Mama." Abby said her vision blurred by tears.

While Abby drove home she thought about the story Roberta had told her. It was exquisitely sweet. When she went into the house, she was pleasantly surprised. Kyle sat in his chair sleeping, a small bundle asleep in each arm. She smiled. Holding their children in his arms didn't detract from Kyle's masculinity, it enhanced it. Abby took her packages to her room to put away. When she finished, she went downstairs to the study. Kyle walked into the study to find Abby sitting behind his desk.

"Where are Kayla and Kerry?" She asked.

"I took them to the nursery." He told her.

"Your desk is a mess. How do you get any work done?" She asked.

"I do paperwork at my office. This is work that doesn't need immediate attention." He said.

"Does your desk at your office look this bad?"

"No, my assistant won't allow it to get this bad."

"Your assistant? Have you forgotten I'm a Legal Assistant?"

"Not anymore you're not. You're my wife. You have the children and this house to take care of. Not to mention me."

"What about me, Kyle? When am I going to have time to do something that fulfills me?"

"You have everything you need to fulfill you." Abby threw her arms in the air and stood up.

"Your mother is right, you are arrogant. You listen to me Kyle Masterson, and you listen well because I'm only going to say this once. I will not sit around and be your ornament. I have a perfectly good degree going to waste. Whether you like it or not I am going to use it." She told him proudly, walking out of the room.

Kyle stood looking at the mess on his desk, mumbling to himself. He could use someone to help with the work he brought home from the office. Could this have been what mother meant when she said to show Abby they belong together? Kin advised including Abby in his plans for the future. Kyle smiled to himself. Going to find Abby, he found her in the kitchen. She heard him coming and pretended to be busy.

"I'm sorry, Querida." He told her wrapping his arms around her from behind, pulling her to his chest. She didn't resist him.

"When we work together the results are very impressive. Look at our children for example." He growled into her ear seductively.

"Is that all you ever think about?" She asked, turning around in his arms.

He answered her question by kissing her deeply. Agnes walked into the kitchen. Kyle looked up. "Go away, Agnes. We're negotiating a business deal." He said lightly.

"I came to tell you I'm going to my sister's. I can see you're busy."

She walked out of the kitchen mumbling about young people and business. "So, do we have a deal?" Kyle asked her.

"Deal? What deal?" She asked.

"Will you be my assistant at home?" He asked, pausing a moment. He pressed his body closer to hers.

~ 237 ~

"Do you mean it, Kyle?" She asked hopefully.

"Of course." He told her, pressing even closer.

Abby punched his shoulder. "You're terrible. I meant do you really want me to be your assistant?"

"I just said so, didn't I? Of course we'll have to work closely together, very closely."

She threw her arms around his neck, kissing both cheeks, then his eyelids. Her kisses covered his entire face.

"Thank you, thank you, thank you." She repeated until his lips claimed hers.

Abby clung to him, pressing closer to relieve her growing, burning hunger. Kyle pressed her against the counter bending her back, forcing her thighs apart with his leg.

"Kyle." She said innocently, melted brown eyes gazing into calm blue ones.

"Yes, Love?" He asked huskily.

"We can't...not here...in the kitchen." She breathed when he pressed his arousal against her.

"Why not?" He said.

"Agnes."

"Went to her sister's. Where's your sense of adventure, Darlin'? Beds aren't the only place for loving."

He kissed her, wiping all sense of propriety from her mind. She wrapped her legs around his waist, forcing him closer. Kyle pulled away when the barrier of their clothes could no longer be tolerated. Abby removed their clothes, pressing their naked bodies closer together. He slipped his fingers inside her satin warmth. She arched into him at the sensual pleasure.

He moved his hands to her waist. She felt his arousal slide inside her. She closed her eyes, pulling him closer with her legs. Kyle tried to pull away.

"No, Kyle, I want you to love me." She demanded.

"Protection." He managed to whisper.

"Already taken care of. She whispered, opening her eyes. "Kiss me, Kyle. Love me now." Abby cried forcing him further inside her.

Unable to resist, he gave into her demands to be loved. Their loving was slow and gentle.

# CHAPTER TWELVE

Kyle came home the next evening to find an eager Abby ready to start work. He'd made her happy when he agreed to let her help with the work at home.

"You're eager this evening." He snapped when she greeted him at the door.

"Bad day at the office." She asked cautiously.

He nodded, holding up his briefcase. "I have a 'ton of work' that has to be done by morning."

"You go to the study. I'll bring supper and a drink for you, then we can tackle your 'ton of work'."

Abby pushed him toward the study. Ten minutes later she pushed a food-laden cart into the study. She had a bottle of Brandy for Kyle.

She poured him a glass. "Here, take this and put something in your stomach." She told him handing him the glass and a plate of food.

"You're going to regret working for me, Sweetheart. I've been told I work like a drudge." He said accepting the food and drink.

"I'm not going to regret anything. Tell me what we're working on." She said, pouring herself a glass of milk.

Kyle explained his work in detail. An hour later Abby had gotten Kyle to eat and they'd made headway on the work he'd brought home. They worked quickly and steadily. She reorganized his desk to hasten their progress. Abby asked Agnes to bring a pot of coffee after Kyle finished his glass of Brandy. Looking over the work they had finished,

Kyle glanced at his watch. Abby was so engrossed in her work she'd lost track of time.

"It's one a.m. Abby. We should go to bed." Kyle said. Abby didn't look up from the papers she was working on. "We can't go to bed until we finish these papers." She said.

"You're worse than I am when it comes to work, Tabitha. Look at me."

He took her chin in one hand, tilting her head up. "We finished the work from my briefcase an hour ago. We've been working on the desk since." He explained.

Abby stood up to stretch her back. "Why didn't you say something? I would have had us here all night trying to finish this." She said waving her hand over the desk.

"I lost track of time myself. Must be the company. I can't remember when I've enjoyed working this much."

"I've enjoyed it too, Kyle. I didn't realize how much I missed working until now."

As the days went by, Abby developed a routine. During the day she cared for her children and the house with Agnes' help. Each evening Kyle came home with a 'ton of work' that had to be done by morning. The days turned into weeks. Abby found her work invigorating. She'd been working because she missed the challenge and enjoyment, not for compensation.

"I can't accept this." Abby told Kyle when he'd produced her first paycheck.

"You are an employee of K. M. Enterprises, Tabitha. I have to compensate you for your time." He told her.

"I'm not working for the money!" She spat.

"Tabitha, you're being unreasonable. Take the check. Throw it away or give it to charity. I don't care what you do with it. You said yourself you have a perfectly good degree. You don't mind using it, why be offended when I offer a salary for the use of it?"

She couldn't come up with a rational response. "I'll take the money, but only for our children and any other children we will have."

Upon seeing the amount of the check, she started to get angry again. Checking her anger, she repeated, "For our children." Kyle laughed.

After receiving her first paycheck she gave the rest over to Kyle to invest. He safely invested them for their children. His heart had skipped a beat when she'd mentioned having more children with him. Each evening Kyle brought home his 'ton of work'. They completed it, and then worked on 'the mess' on his desk.

"You don't like paperwork much do you?" Abby asked one evening.

"What gave me away?" He answered with a question of his own.

Abby gestured at 'the mess', as it had come to be known, on his desk. "This couldn't have accumulated overnight."

"I'd rather work with my employees than do paperwork." He told her.

Abby went to bed blissfully tired at night, content, as Kyle loved her to sleep. She learned more about the man she married as she worked by his side for those few hours each evening. She fell more in love with Kyle as the weeks became months. She was careful not to reveal her love. Kyle hadn't said that he loved her only that he wanted her. Kyle was able to come home earlier and spend more time with his family because of Abby's help. He spent less and less time away from home.

As they worked the months went by. September was upon them; the days began getting cooler. Abby talked to her parents weekly, she'd told them about her job with Kyle.

"When are you coming home for a visit?" Andrew asked.

"I'll ask Kyle when he'll be able to take time off." Abby promised.

Kerry and Kayla were crawling and getting into everything. If Kyle missed a new development in their growth, Abby was quick to tell him about it. She didn't want him to be left out of any part of their lives.

He worked regular hours now. His 'ton of work' was almost nonexistent and 'the mess' had been cleared from his desk.

Kyle came home early one day in September. Abby heard the car and went to investigate.

"Kyle, is something wrong? You're home awfully early." She asked, puzzled.

"My assistant sent me home." He said irritably.

"Kyle, I don't understand. What are you talking about? What's happened?" Abby demanded.

"All the work I've been bringing home, 'the mess' on my desk." He stated.

Abby nodded.

"I've caught up on everything at work. Caroline, my assistant, told me to take a vacation."

"A vacation. That's wonderful, Kyle. We can go to Shelby for a visit."

"I haven't had a vacation in fifteen years. What am I going to do on vacation?"

"Spend time with your family, have fun. Take your wife and children to Shelby." Abby repeated.

Kyle opened his mouth to speak, nothing came out.

Abby threw her arms around his neck, placing kisses all over his face. She laughed at his inability to speak.

"You can help Eric at K. M. Enterprises, Shelby Division."

They went into the house to tell Agnes their plans.

"Agnes." Abby called.

"Yes, Mrs. Masterson." Agnes said coming from the kitchen drying her hands on a towel.

"We're going to Shelby. I'll need you to help pack." Abby told her.

"Yes ma'am." Agnes said.

Abby and Kyle spent the evening making plans for their vacation.

"You won't need to pack much. We can go shopping while we're in Shelby and we'll need to go house hunting while we're there." Kyle told her.

Abby happily made their travel plans. She didn't call her parents to tell them they were coming for a visit. She wanted to surprise them. Agnes helped her pack, asking, "How long will you be away Mrs. Masterson?"

"Kyle said indefinitely when we made our plans. We'll let you know when you can resume your duties here." Abby told her.

"Yes ma'am."

When Kyle's plane landed at the airport Abby could hardly contain her excitement. Kyle helped her take Kerry and Kayla off the plane and put them into their double stroller. As she settled them in, he went to get their luggage and rental car. Abby pushed the stroller to the waiting car. They put Kerry and Kayla into their car seats and the stroller in the trunk. Kyle pulled up in front of her parents' house, beeping the horn. Andrew came to the door after hearing the horn. Looking puzzled, his eyes widened when Abby stepped out of the car.

"It's Tabi." He called to his wife.

Andrew walked out to greet Abby and her family.

"Surprise, Daddy." Abby said throwing her arms around him.

"Welcome home, Tabi." Andrew said with what looked suspiciously like tears in his eyes.

Abby teared up at the emotional response her surprise had caused. Kyle watched as father and daughter greeted one another. He hoped Kayla and Kerry greeted him the same way when they visited him in Atlanta after the divorce.

He had decided to give Abby her divorce after the year was up as agreed. He couldn't live with her knowing she felt trapped in a marriage he'd forced her into.

Clearing his throat, Kyle said, "Hello, Andrew." Andrew took time to recover from his emotions.

"Kyle, good to see you." He said untangling himself from his daughter's arms.

"I'll get the luggage, take the children into the house." Kyle told Abby sharply.

Unexpectedly tears sprang into Abby's eyes at his harsh command. "Kyle?" She said hesitantly.

Ignoring her, Kyle unlocked the trunk. Abby took the stroller from him. Settling the children into it, she took them into the house. "Hi Mama." Abby said when Judy opened the door for her.

Judy helped Abby get the stroller into the house, and then hugged her. "My grandchildren have grown." Judy said emotionally.

Abby laughed. "Yes and they get into anything that isn't nailed down or closed." She said.

Judy laughed too, ushering them into the living room. "How long are you going to stay?" She asked.

"Indefinitely. Kyle doesn't have anything that needs his immediate attention at home." Abby told her.

"We'll have time for a good, long visit." Judy said.

Kyle and Andrew brought the luggage in. Judy told them to put Kerry and Kayla in Abby's old room. Abby settled the children into their portable cribs then went downstairs. Catching up with her parents, she didn't notice how quiet Kyle became. Andrea came home from her date. Upon seeing Abby, she rushed to her, hugging her fiercely.

"I'm glad to see you too, Andie." Abby said.

Pulling away from her sister, Abby looked into her eyes. The haunted look was still there. Before she could comment, Andie said, "How long are you going to be home?" "Indefinitely." Abby answered.

Andrea let out an emotional sigh. "Great, we can stay up all night like when we were kids." She said.

Kyle noticed Andrea referred to Shelby as Abby' s home, the same as Andrew had. He didn't like it, not one bit. Her home was in Atlanta with him.

Abby couldn't hide her yawns behind her hand. Her fatigue was apparent.

"Let's get you to bed, you're exhausted." Kyle said.

She didn't protest when he guided her up the stairs. Once in their room, he pulled her to him. The intensity of his lovemaking shocked her. He dragged her shirt over her head, trapping her arms behind her with the sleeves. Holding her captive, he kissed her until she collapsed against him.

"I want to make love to you, Tabitha. I want to make love to you and make the world go away." He told her desperately.

Kyle gently released her arms from the shirt, letting her go. Abby threw her arms around his neck. Pulling his mouth down to hers, she said, "No Kyle, let me love you."

She kissed him with all the love in her heart. Nothing was going to keep her from showing him her love this night. Abby wouldn't allow him to love her. Like their first night of love, she took control as he had then. She straddled his hips and gently lowered herself onto him. Smiling down into his eyes, she started a slow, easy rhythm.

"Say you love me, Kyle. Tell me we can stay like this forever." She told him with her chocolate brown eyes.

"Step over to the other side, Sweetheart. You can trust your love is in safekeeping." He answered back with clear blue eyes.

Abby closed her eyes, throwing her head back. He arched up as she thrust downward.

"I do love you, Kyle." She told him with her body.

"Say it Darlin'. I love you." He answered.

All through the night they loved each other. Each showed the other how much they were loved through their lovemaking.

After a few days at her parents' Abby could see that Kyle was eager to get to the Shelby office.

"Go into the office, Kyle. The children and I will be fine." Abby told him.

"Are you sure? I don't want you to think I'm abandoning you." Kyle said.

She laughed. "You'd much rather be at the office. You aren't enjoying listening to us gossip. Go to the office, I'll see you tonight." He kissed her, grateful to be doing something besides sitting around the house. When he returned to the house that evening, he was happily exhausted.

"How was your day?" Abby said greeting him at the door.

"Productive. I don't have to do any paperwork. Eric enjoys it." He told her.

"When do you want me to start house hunting?"

"As soon as possible. We'll need the house for our frequent visits to check on the Shelby Division. At least for the first year or so."

Abby began house hunting. After about a month she found the perfect house. When she took Kyle to see it, he loved it as much as she did. After the inspections were complete they signed the papers and began moving in. She spent her days making the house a home.

Kyle became increasingly irritable as their first anniversary drew near. Abby was oblivious to his irritation. She was busy planning Kayla and Kerry's first birthday party. Kyle thought she had forgotten their anniversary.

The day of the birthday party was crisp and cool. Kerry and Kayla were toddling around, getting into the party decorations and trying to get the food. Everyone was enjoying the party. Abby was grateful when the guests finally began to leave. She was glad the party was over. She had scheduled it around the intimate supper she had planned for her first anniversary with Kyle. She hadn't been able to spend time with him all day. First, she'd had to get the arrangements in order for their supper and keep Kyle from learning about her surprise. Second, she had to check on the preparations for the birthday party, and then there had been the party. Judy offered to look after Kerry and Kayla for the weekend so Abby and Kyle could celebrate their anniversary alone.

Abby cleaned up the mess from the party, all the while wondering where Kyle had gone. She went to check on supper, it was ready. She turned everything off. She headed to their room to dress for supper, imagining several lovely surprises Kyle would spring on her for their anniversary. When she walked into their room she did get a surprise, but nothing like she had imagined. Kyle was packing.

"Kyle, what are you doing?" She asked.

"It should be obvious, Tabitha. I'm packing." He said harshly.

"But why? Where are you going?" She asked confused.

"Atlanta." He stated flatly.

"Atlanta, why is there a problem? Wait, I'll go with you. I'll be packed in five minutes." She said dragging her suitcases out of the closet.

Kyle went to her, turning her to face him. "I'm not coming back, Tabitha."

He walked to his dresser. Taking the papers from the top, he walked to Abby, handing them to her. He went back to his packing. Abby took them, a feeling of dread making a sick knot in the pit of her stomach. Reading the papers, tears welled up in her eyes.

"Why, Kyle? You said you'd changed your mind." She said hoarsely.

"You're happy here, Darlin'. I can't sit back and watch you close yourself up again. I don't want to be the cause of your unhappiness by forcing you to stay in this marriage." He said sadly.

"You forced me to marry you. Now you're forcing me to divorce you. What happens if I won't give you a divorce?" She said tonelessly.

He looked at her then. She held the papers in both hands, one on each end.

"What would you do if I tore these papers in half and then tore them in half again?" She hissed, punctuating her speech by doing exactly that.

His knees nearly buckled.

"Tabitha, I'm giving you your freedom. I'm giving you what you've wanted all along." He told her.

"How would you know what I want? You've never bothered to ask me. You threatened me with a custody battle so I'd marry you. Now you're willing to divorce me? Why Kyle?"

"I can't force you to love me. God knows I've tried. I was even fool enough to try a second time to make you jealous. I talked my assistant into loaning me her perfume and lipstick."

"You never said anything about loving me, Kyle. I told you when you first came to Shelby that I wouldn't be jealous over any man, so why the perfume and lipstick?"

"I was trying to make you admit you care, but it backfired."

"God help me I was jealous. I didn't know how to prove I do..." She stopped abruptly, aware of what she'd almost said. She backed away from him, her brown eyes flashing sparks. He slowly advanced toward her until her back was against the wall.

He smiled. "Prove what Tabitha?" He demanded to know.

She tried to move away from the wall, but was effectively trapped in by his hands on either side of her head. She looked everywhere, except at him. He brought his face closer to hers. She looked up and was surprised to see how close he was. His gaze held hers. "Prove what, Tabitha?" He asked again, his mouth only a whisper away from hers.

If she answered him, her lips would be on his. She swallowed the lump in her throat.

"I'm waiting." He was laughing at her.

Fire flashed from her dark brown eyes. "You're laughing at me." She accused.

His smile deepened. "You haven't answered my question, Darlin'." He reminded her.

"I've a good mind not to." She said stubbornly.

"Oh, but you will." He assured her as he pressed his body closer to hers.

"Oh, all right. I love you!" Her voice was strangled by his nearness.

"Say it again."

"I love you." Her declaration was firm.

Kyle stepped away from her. Putting his hands on her waist, he picked her up, twirling her around. Abby put her hands on his shoulders to gather support. He twirled her around until she was dizzy.

"Kyle, put me down. You're making me dizzy."

He set her on her feet. "Do you know how long I've waited to hear you say you love me?"

Abby shook her head.

"Can you imagine how I hated myself for threatening you with a custody battle if you didn't agree to marry me? Or when I had to make you keep your promise to sleep in my bed?"

Abby was so full of emotion she could only shake her head.

"I've been miserable since you left me in Atlanta that first night. I'd found you and lost you all in one night. I love you, Querida." He hugged her to him.

"No Kyle, I am not your mistress."

"My Love, my life, it also means Darling or Dear."

"Kyle Masterson! That was a rotten thing to do."

"All's fair in love and war, Sweetheart."

He kissed her, pulling her toward the bed. They were going to spend their anniversary demonstrating their love.

# EPILOGUE
Three years later

"Mama, Daddy's home, can we open our presents now?" Kayla and Kerry said simultaneously running into the study where Abby was hanging up the phone.

"After I've talked to Daddy. Go into the kitchen and tell Aggie Daddy is home. We'll be along in a few minutes." Abby told them as she stood up.

"We've been waiting all day. And you promised we could open our presents when Daddy came home." Kerry reminded her.

"And you will, after I've talked to Daddy, now scoot." She told them. "Aggie, Aggie, Daddy's home. " Kayla called as she left the study. Abby walked into the living room, picking up two pillows from the sofa. Stuffing them firmly inside her dress, she went to greet her husband. When Kyle saw her, his eyes lit up at the love he saw shining in her eyes. He reached over to pat her 'swollen stomach'.

"Putting on a little weight aren't you, Querida?" He asked. Querida. She'd nearly strangled him when he had finally told her the other ways the word could be translated into English.

"I am putting on a little weight." She admitted.

"You'll have to start exercising if you want to keep eating those delicious desserts Agnes makes." Kyle teased.

"I don't think exercising is going to help keep the weight off. In fact, I'm sure Dr. Cooper will encourage my weight gain." Abby told him smugly.

She watched him closely.

"What does Dr. Cooper have to do with this?" He asked. Abby grinned at him like the cat that ate the canary.

"It's perfectly normal to gain weight in my condition." She informed him.

"Your condition? Querida are you?    "You're pregnant!"

"Yes." She cried throwing herself at him.

"You're sure? You've been to see Dr. Cooper?"  He said, catching her to him.

Abby nodded.

 "When?"

"Today, this morning. I've just finished talking to him."

"No, I meant when is the baby coming?"

"July soon enough for you?"

"July!  We have to get started on the nursery."  He said, setting Abby on her feet.

"Kyle, we have seven months."

"Not if I know you, we don't.  I do not intend to deliver this child.  It is only one, isn't it?"

Abby laughed. "We won't know for a few months yet."

"The nursery will be ready for this baby.  We'll be ready for him or her when he or she decides to make his or her arrival."

"Yes, Kyle." Abby agreed meekly.

"Have you told mother?  She'll spoil this baby as she has Kerry and Kayla.  Have you called your parents?  Andrew has been expecting news that he's going to be a grandfather again." Kyle said.

"Kyle, Daddy does have two other children. I'm sure he doesn't expect us to produce all of his grandchildren. Besides Dr. Cooper and me, you're the only one who knows. I wanted you to be part of this child's life from the beginning."

Kyle pulled her close. "Let's not relive the past. We can't change it, but we can make a better future."

Abby nodded. "Happy Anniversary, Darling."

"Happy Anniversary, Love. What more can a man ask for, a beautiful, loving wife, children who adore him and another baby. No one could be luckier than I am at this moment."

"We'll discuss lucky later. We'd better get into the house before Kayla and Kerry decide we've abandoned them. They've been waiting all day for you to come home. They want to open their birthday presents."

"Daddy, Aggie says if you don't come eat, she's going to throw supper down the garbage disposal." Kerry interrupted.

"Go tell Aggie we'll be in soon, Champ." Kyle told him. Kerry went into the house.

"Do you think they'd miss us if we went to our room first?" Kyle asked huskily.

"Kyle Masterson, you're impossible. Come on, I'm starving."

Kyle allowed Abby to drag him into the house. He laughed at the way she took charge when the circumstances warranted.

He had her for the rest of his life he wouldn't have it any other way.

## Recipe for Abby's Roast and Green Bean casserole

2–3 pound roast
4 cans cream of mushroom soup
4 cans cold water

Preheat oven to 350 degrees. Place roast (thawed or frozen) in large pan, pour soup over top, rinse cans with water, and pour water from cans over roast. Stir and baste, then cover. Put into oven. Cook on 350 degrees for 4–5 hours, (to desired tenderness,) stir and baste every hour. Add water as needed until the last hour of cooking.

2 cans green beans or 1 large bag of thawed frozen green beans
2 cans cream of mushroom soup

Preheat oven to 350 degrees. Drain liquid from beans. Place beans in 2-quart casserole dish. Pour soup over top, rinse cans with water, and pour over beans, stir and cover. Put into the oven. Cook on 350 degrees for approximately one to one and one half hours; stir every 15 minutes.

Badgley Publishing Company

"*Kyle's Passion*" is the first full length novel written by Cassandra J. Sperry. She is also the author of "*A Time to Heal*" and is currently working on her third novel, "*Quinton's Desire*". Each of these novels are linked and could be considered a trilogy, but each tells a unique stand-alone story of love, passion and romance.

These wonderful and powerfully emotional stories are available in all formats. Please visit our website for purchasing options.

**www.BadgleyPublishingCompany.com**